DEADLY SECRETS

A DR HARRISON LANE MYSTERY
BOOK 3

GWYN BENNETT

Storm
PUBLISHING

Copyright © Gwyn Bennett, 2021, 2023

The moral right of the author has been asserted.

To request permissions, contact the publisher at rights@stormpublishing.co

Ebook ISBN: 978-1-80508-007-7
Paperback ISBN: 978-1-80508-008-4

Cover design: Tash Webber
Cover images: Unsplash

Published by Storm Publishing.
For further information, visit:
www.stormpublishing.co

ALSO BY GWYN BENNETT

1

The music thumped across the beach, drowning out the sound of the incoming tide. Riton and Nightcrawlers' beat was accompanied by a host of out-of-tune voices shouting, 'It's Friday then...' which quickly degenerated into a mash of forgotten, or too-drunk-to-sing, lyrics. The party was firmly nestled within the sand dunes, well away from any potential complaining neighbours on the north-eastern coast of England, and just over an hour's coach drive from Durham. It was well organised. A huge bonfire had been lit, ready for when the two coaches full of University students had arrived, while a generator provided power for the music.

The bar was a big free-for-all pile of everything alcoholic you could think of. Several plastic bins were labelled 'Moathouse Monks Mead' and were filled with a reddy-brown liquid that tasted of nothing more than fruit juice with a hint of honey, but would have you over the limit to drive with just three sips. Luckily nobody there was planning on driving home.

The two coach drivers were sitting well away from the revelry, discussing the behaviour of their passengers, while nursing a warm coffee in the mid-October evening. Their conversation was interrupted by two female students giggling and tripping down one of the sand dunes in front of them. Under the light of the moon, the two men watched as the pair started to take each other's clothes off, giggling and kissing, oblivious to their audience. It was tempting to let them carry on, but Derek, who had three teenage daughters at home, stood up and reached in through his driver's door, turning on the engine and flooding the dunes in front of them with headlights. The pair didn't seem that bothered, but ran off back towards the party, laughing.

There were others like them, peeled off from the main group, making out in the dunes, but most of the sixty students danced around the big bonfire, plastic drink glasses in hand, shouting, singing.

At the stroke of midnight, the music stopped. A few in the group knew what was about to happen, but most of them were oblivious, as figures in black cloaks appeared around the surrounding dunes. They were chanting 'Timeo enim Deus vester ipse est hic in nobis, Timeo enim Deus vester ipse est hic in nobis' over and over. The others started to join in, watching as the monks stood atop the dunes, hands clasped together piously, looking down on them all.

Soon the stragglers had re-joined the group around the fire, ready for the main event, everyone chanting together as one. 'Timeo enim Deus vester ipse est hic in nobis...' their voices entwined with the whispers of the sea as its waves dragged back down the beach.

Then one monk turned and disappeared, before returning with a pig. Several of the girls in the group gasped and cried out as they saw the silver blade of the knife in his hand.

For a moment, there was silence.

'For Bacchus and Venus,' the black-cloaked figure shouted, and turned, plunging the knife down towards the pig.

More of the girls squealed in shock.

The monks disappeared.

There was chattering, and the pitch of shocked voices around the firelight, as the silence of the night held them all stunned.

They didn't wait long. Within seconds, a black line of monks trooped into the gathering carrying enormous platters of hog roast pork and bread rolls. The shock turned to laughter again as they heard the squealing of the indignant but unharmed pig being loaded back into a truck to be taken away by the muttering farmer. They had paid him well for their fun.

The music resumed as the party-goers helped themselves to the hog roast, watched by the masked, hooded monks. All the young men were waiting to see if they would be chosen. This was a preference party, when those who would go forward for the selection dinner to become a Moatside Monk, the most sought-after new student dining society in Durham, were chosen. Tonight, just two would receive the invites – their chance to join the elite and become one of the brotherhood. Plenty of money was a prerequisite, titles and the right schooling helped too, but there was more to being a monk than that. They'd all been watched throughout the evening to see if they fitted the club's criteria. No one knew who was a Monk already, although some had their suspicions. What they did know, was that becoming a Monk was a lifelong pledge, a vow of secrecy in return for a brotherhood that would help you throughout your career; an invisible hand to lift you to the highest echelons of society – and guarantee the best dinner parties you'd ever been to.

Only a few had been to the preference party before. But there was just one who wasn't laughing or drinking with the others. They watched in the shadows, away from the bonfire. Horrified. Not because of the fake pig sacrifice, or the drinking, but because they couldn't believe it was all taking place again, exactly as last year. After what had happened, did they not learn their lesson? Feel some guilt? Had he been forgotten so easily? Even the chant showed they still thought themselves above all laws, earthly and heavenly: *Fear your God, for he is here among us.*

There was one Monk in particular who thought himself a god, untouchable. It couldn't be allowed to happen again. The Moatside Monks had to pay for their past sins.

2

The roadworks site manager rushed over and looked as if he was about to hug Dr Harrison Lane as he got off his Harley Davidson bike. Thankfully, it was just an emotional feeling, which he kept to himself and didn't put into practice.

'Dr Lane, I'm so glad to see you. They've downed tools and won't get back to work, it's costing the company a fortune. We're behind schedule already and I'm getting it in the neck from my boss. I need you to tell them it's all rubbish, persuade them they're not going to be cursed.'

The orange high-vis jacket he wore added an extra hue to his already flushed face, and he seemed unable to stand still for even a few seconds. Harrison didn't need to be a psychologist to know that Max Fuller was stressed.

They were at a major crossroads in London, or at least, what should be a major intersection. Right now it was a roadworks site devoid of any workers, and all around them the scowling faces of daily commuting traffic were being re-routed in the opposite direction. At the far end of the site,

Harrison could see a large huddle of men who looked like a group of frightened school boys. In the middle, a police car had pulled up and a uniformed officer stood peering into a large hole.

'The pathologist is coming,' Max continued. It seemed to help him to talk and wave his hands around. 'We're supposed to have a roundabout built in the next five days. I just don't know what to say to them. This isn't going to take too long, is it?'

Harrison ticked off all the textbook signs of anxiety and felt for the man. He was only in his early thirties, and clearly out of his depth. Lewisham police had put in the call to Harrison. As head of the Ritualistic Behavioural Crime unit, this wasn't his usual kind of case. He was pretty certain it wasn't going to be a recent death, but the response of the work crew and the impact it was having on London's traffic flow warranted an immediate response in the public interest.

They walked towards the uniformed police officer and the large hole.

'Any history about this site?' Harrison asked Max Fuller.

He shrugged. His brain was probably incapable of recalling much right now, but Harrison thought it was worth a try.

'Plans showed there'd been a crossroads here for forever. It was enlarged over the years and now they want a roundabout.'

'OK.'

Max stared at him, searching his face for some reassurance, but Harrison never made empty promises. He needed to look at the facts first.

A ladder was leaning against the edge of the hole, which was around four metres deep and fifteen metres wide. At the bottom, Harrison saw the object causing all the fuss disruption and distress – its yellowed bones contrasting with the dark, almost black soil around it. He noted the broken stake through its torso, where a heart would have been, and the decapitated skull between its legs. Harrison could hear from the voices which reached his ears that most of them were Eastern European, where superstitions were more deeply believed and vampire legends part of folklore.

Harrison looked around the site. It was difficult to tell exactly where the old crossroads would have been, but the buildings surrounding it gave him some indications. The footprint of their foundations had probably not changed too much over the years – although they wouldn't have even existed when this person found their way into the soil.

He was pretty sure about what he was looking at already, but climbed down into the hole, more for show in front of the men than anything else. If he was to persuade them that he knew what he was talking about, he needed to look as though he'd done a thorough inspection.

The bones and skull showed significant age. They were yellowed and pitted, and the body wasn't lying neatly on its back, but looked more haphazard in its placement, as though little care had been put into its burial. It was the placing of the skull which gave Harrison the biggest clue. He wasn't an expert in archaeological remains, but he knew what beliefs people had put into practice over the centuries.

'You can cancel the pathologist,' Harrison said to Max as he climbed back out of the hole. 'The victim has been dead for hundreds of years,' he added with a wry smile. 'You'll be wasting their time. You need a forensic anthropologist. I'd contact the Museum of London Archaeology unit if I were you.' He nodded towards the large group of men, who were all watching him intently. 'Will they understand me, or do you have an interpreter?'

'The foreman will interpret anything that's needed,' Max confirmed, reaching for his mobile phone. 'Archaeologists? Don't they take like forever to dig over things?'

Harrison didn't reply. That was one stress he couldn't help with and left Max to report back while he walked over to the group of around twenty-five labourers. They were all dressed in high-vis jackets and carried the weather-beaten look of men who were used to working outdoors. They looked pretty tough – not the sort you'd want to cross in a bar fight – but right now their superstitions had reduced them all to a fearful gaggle who looked at the tall, muscular man approaching them in black bike leathers with a mix of distrust and hope. Close on Harrison's heels came the police officer, who was interested in hearing what he had to say. Max followed up the rear.

'My name is Dr Harrison Lane, I am head of the Metropolitan Police's Ritualistic Behavioural Crime unit,' he started, allowing a brief pause for the interpreter to repeat his words. 'The skeleton which you uncovered this morning is from the Middle Ages, probably around six hundred to seven hundred years old. The reason it was placed in the way you found it is because they probably committed a serious crime, such as murder. In those times, they sometimes hung the accused, after execution, in cages at crossroads for all to see the punishment. It was called gibbeting. The bodies were then disposed of nearby, away from consecrated ground. Christians at the time believed that in order to rise from the dead on Judgement Day, a body had to be whole. This is why the head has been severed and placed between his legs. They were denying him that opportunity and ensuring a bad man didn't walk again. The stake through his torso is a little extra insurance. This is not a vampire burial. There are no items placed in the jaw of the skull as we have seen in suspected vampire burials in Europe. There are no curses associated with burials like this. He is merely a man who was not well thought of, disposed away from holy ground because of a crime he committed in life.'

Harrison stopped for a moment as the interpreter caught up and the group of men responded to his words with murmurs and other noises of apprehension. Behind him, the police officer *hmphed* in appreciation.

'I know this,' continued Harrison, 'because there have been other bodies found in the same way in London. Recently there was one in St Mary Spital. You have nothing to fear from this burial. An archaeologist will come and take the remains away.'

Someone asked the interpreter something.

'They want to know if you're sure it is not vampire,' the interpreter translated to Harrison.

'I'm sure. A vampire wouldn't have been buried at a cross-roads like this. This is someone who they wanted to punish and show everyone what happens if you commit crimes like they did.'

'But the stake?' the man pressed.

'It was merely a superstition among some to prevent violent criminals from rising again on Judgement Day. This person had his judgement here on earth and uncovering him will not change the fact his head is no longer attached. He cannot come back to haunt you. He is unable to rise. His executors made sure of that.'

The interpreter nodded at Harrison's words and repeated them back to the waiting men. He seemed placated, which boded well, hopefully he'd persuade the others. A few moments later, Harrison could almost feel the collective wave of relief flow through them. There was much discussion in their native tongue, but the mood was positive.

Harrison looked at his watch and turned to Max.

'I have to go. Get the archaeology team from MOLA here, they'll take him away. I think they'll probably agree with what I've just said.'

'It's crazy. I can't believe they think it might be a vampire,' Max said.

'Fear has many deep-rooted causes,' Harrison replied, 'and superstitions and folklores have been passed down for generations. In their minds, it is a possibility and not fiction.'

With that, he headed back to his bike. He had a meeting with Detective Sergeant Jack Salter to get to in order to put to rest some fears of his own.

3

'Here he is, the vampire slayer of Lewisham,' DS Jack Salter laughed out loud at his own joke – a trait he was fond of, but it also raised a few smiles and smirks from the team around him. Harrison knew it wasn't meant in disrespect, he'd worked with Jack enough times now to brush his humour off.

The blond-haired DS was sitting at his desk, a half-eaten ham and cheese roll in front of him, and a drunk takeaway coffee cup and croissant wrapper in his bin; evidence he'd been there for a while already.

Harrison thought Jack's face looked more relaxed, and like he may have gained a kilo or two in the last few weeks. That was a positive. They were in the Major Investigation Team incident room at Europe's largest purpose-built police station. Harrison recognised many of the faces, plus a few fresh ones. There was a low-level hum of activity around them. Officers on the phone, fingers typing on keyboards. He could usually tell what stage an investigation was at by the activity levels in the room. Harrison glanced over at Jack's boss's office. Detective Chief Inspector Sandra Barker wasn't in residence.

'Sounds like you got your teeth into the problem,' Jack said to him. 'Hope it wasn't a pain in the neck.' The suspected vampire had been the talk of Lewisham police station that morning and every vampire joke in the book had been aired.

'It's hundreds of years old, not a police matter,' Harrison replied, keen to get on, and thankfully Jack also knew him well enough to know that he wasn't being rude. It was just his way.

'Right, Inspector Morgan is due in ten minutes. Let's head downstairs.' Jack grabbed the last of his roll and it disappeared in two mouthfuls. He screwed the wrapper into a ball and threw it into Sergeant Steve Evans' bin en route.

'In one, Taff,' Jack said to the Welsh sergeant, who had put his hand up for a congratulatory high five.

Harrison was glad to follow Jack out of the incident room. He was getting that feeling again, the same one he'd had when they'd gone to visit the sister of the Nunhead cemetery murder victim. It was a dark shadow just behind his shoulder. He could feel it, cold and foreboding. Its breath sent shivers down his spine and made his neck and shoulder stiffen. He wanted to know the truth, but something told him to run.

'So, Inspector Morgan was a PC in 2004, at the time of your mother's death.' Jack left the joviality of the incident room behind them and briefed him on the way down the stairs. 'He worked out of Carmarthen, which you may remember is about ten minutes from where you both lived. Obviously he was only a junior at the time, but when I spoke to him on the phone a couple of weeks ago, he had some interesting things to say. I'm hoping we might be able to pull enough evidence together to re-open the case soon.'

Harrison said nothing as they exited the stairs. His mind was in Carmarthenshire. From the miles upon miles of fields and the vast stony landscape of the Brecon Beacon mountains, with its fairy and dragon legends, to the county town of Carmarthen, home of Merlin. It was a beautiful place, but it brought back dark memories. Things he had tried hard to bury, but which were about to be split open.

'I thought we could go to Maggie's, get us a coffee and some privacy— Here he is...' Jack said to Harrison.

They walked into the reception area of Lewisham police station and Jack headed towards a man who sported more hair on his face than he possessed on his head. Harrison strained to see behind the thick brown beard. Did he recognise the police officer in front of him? His mind was blank.

'DS Salter, Dr Lane,' Inspector Morgan held out his hand in greeting and returned Harrison's stares with his own intense gaze. 'I'm pleased to see you've done well,' he added to Harrison. 'Last time I saw you, you were in a bad way. It was a big shock for a young lad to deal with.'

Flashbacks of an angry eighteen-year-old raging at the police came into Harrison's mind. He hadn't handled any situation well in those days, let alone that one. He didn't recognise the young man he'd been back then, and he pitied anyone who'd tried to deal with him.

'I wasn't much older than Dr Lane myself,' he said to Jack, 'not long out of police college and hoping to change the world.' He smiled wryly to himself. 'That case introduced me to the reality that it wasn't going to be as simple as identifying who or what was good or bad.'

It was a strange feeling for Harrison. He'd spent seventeen years believing he was the only one who would ever think of his mother's death as murder and not suicide. Now, he might have another witness from that time to corroborate his view. It was almost unbelievable. He was grateful to Jack for trusting in him and looking into the case. Jack had already identified inconsistencies with the investigation and evidence. Now, they had a serving police officer who had been there at the time.

As they walked to the cafe, Harrison following the two men as they gossiped about another colleague they'd both worked with, Harrison wondered if Inspector Morgan knew what had happened to him after the inquest recorded the suicide verdict. Perhaps he would avoid the subject, save Harrison any awkwardness. Either way, it didn't matter. He had left that young man behind a long time ago.

Inspector Morgan gave a quizzical glance at Harrison's herbal tea as they all sat down in Maggie's. He had a large cappuccino in front of him, into which he deposited two heaped teaspoons of sugar and proceeded to stir it rhythmically. Jack flopped onto the green leather bench next to Harrison, facing Inspector Morgan. He pocketed his wallet and took out his notebook to signal they were getting down to business.

'Firstly, thank you again, Inspector, for taking time to talk to us today,' he started.

'Please, it's Rob, call me Rob.'

'Would you like to tell us what you remember about the case, Rob?'

'Sure. I was young, a rookie, but they had assigned me a more experienced partner to learn from, Sergeant Christopher Jones, and we were first on scene. You weren't there at that point,' he said, nodding to Harrison. 'I think you'd gone away for a couple of nights and didn't get back until we'd contacted you.'

Harrison gave a small nod of his head in agreement.

'We found Isabel Lane. She was already deceased, hanging in a barn, which I believe was used by the commune for meetings. On first look, my partner and I both felt that it wasn't a suicide. There was no obvious way for her to have climbed up there for one thing, no kicked-away chair or stool. Plus, there was bruising on her arms and you could just see some marks on her face. We called it in as suspicious.'

'What happened then?' Jack asked.

'We started interviewing the rest of the group. It was led by a Desmond and Freda Manning – I'm not sure which one of them I disliked the most. Both of them made me feel uneasy. They seemed to have an influence over all the others there. No one would say or do anything without their agreement. It felt like a cult. My partner said we would have to take the Mannings out of the situation, interview them at the station to separate them from the others, and that was the only way we'd get to the truth. It was a good call, but unfortunately didn't happen.'

'Oh?' queried Jack.

'The boss arrived. Chief Superintendent Morris Lewis. He was a couple of years out from retirement, which couldn't come soon enough in most of our views. He had a word with Chris, my partner, and after that it became a suicide.'

'Didn't you query it?'

'Of course I did. Couldn't understand the sudden change when it was obvious that something wasn't right. Chris wouldn't discuss it. Told me to drop it if I wanted a career in the police force. He was angry about it, I could tell. Next thing I know, a stool appeared in the barn and that became evidence that she'd taken her own life. That along with the testimony of group members who all reported that she'd been depressed and suicidal beforehand. I'm sorry,' he said, looking at Harrison, 'I was young, out of my depth. I didn't understand what had just gone on and so I kept quiet.' Rob Morgan looked down at his coffee. 'It's haunted me all my career. I knew it was wrong, that Lewis had pulled rank and shut us down, but how could a new PC do anything about that?'

'Any ideas why Chief Superintendent Lewis did it?'

'I saw him talking to the Mannings. It wasn't friendly, they weren't chatting like mates. They had something on him, I know it. But I've no idea what. Either way, he was in their pockets. He looked uncomfortable around them and after-wards, there was no discussion about the investigation.'

'Did you have any theories as to why Isabel would have been murdered?' Jack asked Rob.

'No. I just know that not long after, they all disappeared. I think they'd gone even before the inquest. None of them turned up for it.'

'I think they killed her because we were going to leave,' said Harrison. 'I think she'd been living there under duress for a while, but it was like she put up with it while I was with her. It was odd because on the one hand she seemed to protect me from them, yet she didn't seem to contemplate taking us out of the situation until I'd become eighteen. I think they also had some kind of hold over her. Maybe she found something out about them too.' He looked at Rob and Jack, who were studying him closely. He found it hard to voice his thoughts, and he didn't like the undertone of sympathy in their eyes, so he stopped.

'There was definitely more to them than what they

appeared,' agreed Rob. 'I heard other rumours too about how they had various people, all around the country, in their pockets. Nothing concrete though, no names or any idea of what it could relate to.'

'Is Lewis still around?' Jack asked.

Rob shook his head. 'He popped his clogs ages ago, massive stroke. No great loss, that one. Unfortunately, Chris is also gone; prostate cancer. I'm not sure how many others who were on the Force then might know anything. Might be worth digging around. What about the Mannings? You found them?'

'They found me,' Harrison said, his jaw clenching.

Rob frowned.

'We don't know where they are right now,' Jack added, 'but we will find them again. We need to gather as much evidence as possible and get this case reopened. We also believe they were responsible for the murder of a young woman in Nunhead Cemetery in 1993.'

'I'll help all I can,' said Rob. 'It would be good to see this put right after so long.'

Harrison had watched Rob Morgan closely throughout the conversation. He seemed genuine. There were no signs of stress. His breathing was regular and eye contact steady. He didn't hesitate in his answers. This was a man who they could rely on, and who was telling the truth.

Jack took as much detail and as many names as Rob could supply down in his notebook. It would be a slow process checking them all out, especially as he was doing it in his spare time, but Harrison knew he'd be thorough.

After four cappuccinos and two mint teas between them, they were done, and it was time for Rob to head off back to Gloucestershire where he now lived and worked.

'I meant it, it's good to see you've made something of your life and not allowed what happened to dominate it,' Rob said warmly to Harrison as he left.

Harrison thanked him but didn't mention that, on the contrary, what happened had dominated his life and career and would continue to do so. His entire focus was on finding and catching the Mannings and anyone else like them, and he felt they were getting tantalisingly close.

4

Harrison didn't feel like making small talk on the way back to the station, not that he indulged in small talk at the best of times, but right now he really wanted to be alone to allow the last hour's conversation to sink in. He did, however, know that he owed Jack a debt of gratitude. He didn't need to do this for him, put in time outside of his own job, and he appreciated it.

'How are Marie and Daniel?' Harrison asked.

Jack smiled. That was a good sign.

'They're good. Daniel is trying to crawl, which means we're going to need to start baby-proofing the house, but he's also a lot more fun now. He babbles away to his toys, nothing coherent but no worse than me after a good night out. Marie's on pretty good form too. That trip to her parents really helped. She still gets the odd bad couple of days, but she's started socialising with other mums now.'

'That's a huge improvement,' Harrison replied. 'Means she's gained confidence about her mothering skills. A couple of months back you couldn't even get her to go out of the house.'

'I know, and yeah, it's good. Those first months were...' Jack didn't finish his sentence. He didn't need to. Harrison knew he'd been to hell and back with Marie's postnatal depression, but the main thing was they were putting it behind them all. It also explained why he looked less stressed and had put on those extra couple of kilos.

'I'd better get my arse back to my desk before the boss notices,' Jack said as they reached the station, and with a hand raise, ducked inside.

Harrison also needed to head back to his office and was on the way to being reunited with his Harley Davidson, when he saw Jack's boss, DCI Sandra Barker, in the car park. She was talking on her mobile and looked a little upset, pacing back and forth. He thought it best to give her some privacy, but she saw him and waved for him to hold on while she finished her call.

Harrison looked away. It was hard for him not to analyse people and their mannerisms and expressions. Occasionally, like now, he felt like he was intruding, because his mind immediately began to examine every gesture for clues as to what was going on in her mind. She'd clearly come outside, away from the office, to prevent anyone else from doing the same. Instead, Harrison concentrated on checking his emails on his phone.

'Harrison, how are you?' Sandra asked as she walked up to him. DCI Barker was in her fifties, with a dark-blonde, grey-streaked bob, but otherwise barely looked her age. She'd managed to avoid any middle-aged spread, despite her well-known passion for chocolate. While she probably never got her full eight hours of sleep a night, today she looked slightly more pinched than usual, with dark circles under her eyes.

'Fine, and you?'

'So-so. Got a few stresses going on at home. Gemma has gone to uni and I think she's homesick. That was her just now. Sam thinks she should be having the time of her life, but I just don't think she wants to do the things he did when he was a student. There are so many expectations. It's been just a few weeks, but do you have any advice on how to ease separation anxiety? For her and us.' Sandra smiled as she said it, but Harrison knew her well enough to see past it. She dealt with hardened criminals and some of the results of their worst crimes, and was a dedicated officer, putting in way over the regular hours. She valued and fought for every one of her team, but her family were number one and she never lost sight of that, even if she struggled to spend the time with them that she should.

'What is she doing or saying that makes you think she's anxious?'

'She keeps ringing me up, for one thing. When she's at home, I only hear from her when she needs something. Now, it's every day, sometimes more than once a day.'

'Is she worried about anything in particular? Or mentioning something or someone?'

'Not really. She said she's happy with her course, has made some good friends, but something's not right.'

'That's a great sign already. It's quite normal for students to feel a little homesick when they first go away. It usually lasts a few weeks and then they settle into their new lives. Going to university is a big change – a completely new environment, surrounded by new people. The phone calls are her way of staying connected with and comforted by the familiar

when facing the unknown. She'll find her feet soon enough,'
he reassured.

'I hope so.'

'Where has she gone?'

'Durham.'

'An excellent university, she'll be fine, just give her time.'

'Yeah, I'm sure she will.' Sandra pressed her lips together.
Harrison knew that was a sign she was trying to keep her
anxiety under control. She changed the subject. 'Good work
on the roadworks vampire, by the way. The media have gone
crazy for it, wanted to speak to the man who persuaded the
workmen to get back on the job.'

Harrison held his hands up in horror to say *no*.

'It's OK, I knew what your response would be. Lee
Matthews, that forensic anthropologist from MOLA, has
jumped on it. Fancies himself as a TV presenter and is gagging
for media attention. You can stay in the background. You're
more valuable to us anyway if you do. Got to get back. Take care.'

Harrison smiled at the fast disappearing back of DCI
Barker. She had been one of a tiny handful to believe in him
when he'd first started the unit. He'd often wondered if he'd
still be doing this job if it wasn't for her support.

HARRISON'S 'UNIT', which admittedly only consisted of him
and his analyst, Ryan Chapman, was buried deep in the
bowels of New Scotland Yard. When he pushed open the
door to his office, he was met by the sight of Ryan staring
intently at a large rubber toad.

'Boss,' the young man said to him, placing it onto his
desk. 'A toad just arrived in the post. There's a note with it

from DCI Whittaker, said it was a little momento for your work with them in Cambridgeshire.'

'That was the jockey's body found on the Fens.'

'I thought he was a Horseman,' Ryan replied, returning to his own desk.

'He was, but linked to the old Toadmen and their customs. They all had toad bones round their necks.

'You can add him to the collection then.' Ryan smirked at the toad and the shelves around their office which was a mini museum to all things occult, mythical, and spiritual. Along the walls were various artefacts from cases over the years, including voodoo dolls, skulls and spell books.

Ryan was in his late twenties, overweight, and the colour of his skin indicated he hadn't seen sunlight for some time. The fact they worked out of a basement office with no windows partially explained this away, but it was also indicative of Ryan's overall allergy to fresh air, exercise, and healthy food. He and Harrison were two opposites. Junk food was an improvement on Ryan's original intake of choice, but Harrison was concerned that too was starting to take its toll. He worried that Ryan had replaced an illegal drug with a legal one which could still have an impact on his health, albeit less dramatically. He was about to suggest he buy them both lunch, when a sharp knock sounded on the office door, and it was pushed open to reveal a grey-haired man in a suit. He looked like he wouldn't have been out of place in one of the old-fashioned spy movies, apart from the fact the suit had a modern cut and he carried an iPad along with a A4 white envelope.

'Dr Harrison Lane?' the man asked.

'Yes. Leo Fawcett?' Harrison replied.

The man's face registered surprise before the mask of authority returned.

'That's correct. Yes. Leo Fawcett, Operations with the National Crime Agency.'

Harrison could see he wanted to ask him how he knew who he was, but for now Fawcett had gone for composure rather than inquisitiveness.

'We have been trying to contact you, Dr Lane. I appreciate you're a busy man, but there have been some discussions between the Met and the NCA and I wanted to talk to you about them.'

He waited for Harrison to respond, but when the silence lasted more than a few seconds, he seemed compelled to prompt him.

'I wonder if we could talk in private?'

'Yeah, well, I was heading off to get some lunch anyways,' Ryan said, throwing a glance at Harrison. Harrison caught the flicker of worry on his face. Ryan knew full well that Leo Fawcett had been trying to get hold of him for weeks, and why. While he'd done his best to ignore the inevitable, it had finally arrived.

'Thanks, Ryan,' he said. Trying to give him a reassuring look. 'Take a seat, Mr Fawcett,' he added to his uninvited guest, and lifted a stack of magazines from a chair. He loaded them onto his desk instead. 'Leo, please,' he replied as he sat down and eyed the magazines Harrison had just moved. They weren't the usual titles found in a doctor's surgery. *Spirituality Studies*, *The Journal for the Study of Religion*, and *The Journal of Forensic Psychology Practice* were likely to be harder reading than *GQ* or *Esquire*. *The Paranormal Review* also caught his interest. He resisted the urge to pick it up and flick through to read, 'Images of the Occult', and 'The Family

Backgrounds of Highly Psychic Adults', and instead turned his attention back to Harrison.

'You were expecting me then?' he asked.

Harrison knew he was referencing how he'd realised who he was.

'You called several times. I recognised your voice from the messages, and I saw the NCA logo on that envelope you're holding.'

Leo Fawcett smiled.

'I was told you don't miss much,' he replied. He seemed to relax once he knew Harrison hadn't used some strange mind-reading powers. 'Unusual decor,' he added, nodding towards the wall of artefacts.

'All from past cases,' Harrison replied. 'So has the decision been made?' He was already tired of the preamble and wanted to cut to the chase.

'Decision? Well, yes, it has to a certain extent, but I wanted to see you in person to discuss your options. This is a positive for you, Dr Lane. For one thing, you can have an office with some natural light.' He tried to soften the mood, aware the meeting was taking the tone of a redundancy announcement. 'You have a special set of skills which are being increasingly used by police forces around the UK, not just the Met. You are a very valuable asset, Dr Lane, and you belong with the National Crime Agency, where we can utilise your skills for the benefit of the whole country. While we recognise the foresight of the Met in starting this unit, you have without doubt proven that it is both necessary and highly effective in solving cases.'

'That's one thing I want to clarify,' Harrison interrupted. 'You are talking about my unit, or just me? Ryan is an intrinsic part of my work. Does your proposal include him?'

'We do have our own highly trained research analysts at the NCA,' Leo began, and then, seeing the look on Harrison's face, quickly changed tack. 'But if you require your assistant's particular skill set, then yes, of course, the proposal includes him.'

Harrison nodded in acceptance and waited for him to continue.

'There will be a pay rise, and although the chain of command will change, we expect you to work in much the same way as you do now. You also don't necessarily need to move if you don't want to. We can give you a base here in London or at Foxley Hall in Hampshire. I anticipate you will travel around the country a fair amount.' Leo paused a moment to see if Harrison wanted to ask a question, and then continued.

'I want to reassure you that apart from your job title changing from Ritualistic Behavioural Crime Unit with the Met, to the RBCU with the NCA, there will be very little change, but you will get access to a lot more resource. This is a very positive step, a recognition of your work, Dr Lane.'

Leo Fawcett sat back, his sales pitch done, and he waited. There was no indication as to how Harrison had taken the news. His face was unreadable. Harrison's eyes dropped to the envelope on the desk next to Leo.

'This is more detail for you.' Leo Fawcett took the prompt. 'Perhaps you want to take some time to think about what we've discussed and read through it. If you have any questions, I'm available 24/7.'

Harrison rose from his chair and reached his hand out across the desk. It was a clear signal that the meeting was over.

'Thank you for taking the time to come to see me, Leo. I

look forward to you confirming the position regarding Ryan and I assume that the pay rise will also relate to his salary. I'll be back in touch once we have received that confirmation.'

Leo Fawcett realised that Ryan's salary was a statement rather than a question. Dr Harrison Lane drove a hard bargain, but it was a request which would be met. They needed Harrison Lane on the team. His track record made that very clear, and he'd been told to secure his services whatever the cost.

A long the bank of the River Wear, a pounding beat spilled out of Klute nightclub, contrasting with the gentle flow of the river. The Wear meandered around the heart of Durham, where Durham Cathedral and Castle rose up from their bed of sandstone.

Two students were stood out the back of the infamous Klute – which was known as the worst nightclub in Europe, but beloved by Durham University's student body – on Elvet bridge, staring down at the dark river in a semi-drunk state. They were freshers, two lads from Cumbria and Yorkshire, who had been making the absolute most of their new freedom. Both of them were proud of the fact they'd been drunk every single night since arriving, but it was catching up on them. They were contemplating the walk back up the hill to Van Mildert College, and discussing the option of heading back into town first to get a kebab. It was just gone 1 a.m., and they hadn't yet worked out what takeaways would still be open.

They were about to go off in search of food when one of them spotted a rowing boat that was floating along on its own. At first, he thought it was empty. The dark shape of the figure lying inside it merged with the boat's interior in the gloom of night. As it passed under the bridge, there was just enough light to make out the form of a person.

'Oi, mate!' he shouted down. 'Wake up.'

'What you on about?' His friend, turned back to see why he was shouting at him to wake up.

'There's a guy fallen asleep in a boat.' He pointed down to the river and rushed across to the other side of the bridge to look for the boat, which had disappeared underneath them.

Both lads leaned over the stone bridge, peering at the water, and were rewarded by the sight of the boat, oar-less, floating out from under the bridge. The person still asleep and seemingly unaware of the danger they were in.

'Hey, hey, wake up! Wake up. Somebody help, there's a man in that boat!'

At this point, luck played its hand. Two Durham constabulary PCs were strolling a couple of hundred yards away, and had only just remarked on how peaceful everything seemed. They responded instantly to the shouts and joined the two students in leaning over the edge of the bridge. The boat was drifting well away from them by now, but one officer used his torch to shine in the boat – mainly because he could smell the alcohol on the breath of the two lads and wasn't convinced about what they thought they had seen. Within seconds he was on his radio and alerting colleagues that someone could be in danger.

The boat had drifted quite a way downstream before the fire services' water rescue team could secure it and pull it to the bank. At first the crew and officers thought they'd wasted their time; a student prank, tricked by a dummy dressed in a black hooded cloak. It was only when a police officer pulled the hood back that they all realised they were, in fact, looking at a corpse. A young man dressed in a monk's black habit and cowl, who was decidedly dead.

6

Harrison was meeting his mentor and friend, Professor Andrew McKendrick for dinner. They had a table booked at one of Andrew's favourite restaurants, a little family-run Italian in Wimbledon. To save the cost of a cab, and so Andrew could have a couple of glasses of his favourite tipple, Barolo, Harrison was picking him up from his house on his Harley. Andrew always said it made him feel like a young rebel when he got on the back of his bike.

Andrew lived in a Victorian terraced house in Balham, south London. He'd lived there for as long as Harrison had known him, although the condition and decor of the house had changed considerably over that time. In Harrison's student years it had been an eclectic mishmash of 1970s and 80s style with a veneer of original Victorian features.

In those days Andrew had found his mortgage took up most of his salary, leaving little for refurbishment. Now, the monthly payments were a snip compared to the London property values and his salary. With no family to spend his

hard-earned cash on, Andrew had instead spent a good
chunk of it on his home. It was a large house for just one
man. Spread across three floors, he had a good-sized sitting
room on the ground floor, with a large kitchen-diner. His
favourite room was the office, filled with mementos from his
many research trips around the world. It would also
undoubtedly be the best place to hide in the event of nuclear
attack, because of the floor-to-ceiling stacks of books which
lined the entire room. He and Harrison had spent many
evenings in there pulling books off shelves and quoting theories and scriptures to each other as they pondered the
mysteries and foundations of the world's religions.

Harrison had occasionally wondered why Andrew never
married. He was a good guy, attractive enough to have had his
fair share of student crushes, although nowadays those were
thankfully thin on the ground. The age gap had got just too
large for even the most besotted groupie to venture there.
Harrison had never brought the subject up about his single
status. He was hardly in a position to comment on someone
else's lack of relationships, when he had his own aversion to
intimacy and commitment.

He hadn't seen Tanya since last Sunday. They'd ended up
having a fantastic day out of town. Harrison had gone round
to her flat in the morning and they'd talked about going to
one of the big museums in London, or for a walk in the park.
Just being with her was a pleasant enough way to spend the
day, but Tanya had always wanted to see the Ashmolean
Museum in Oxford, so Harrison told her to jump on the back
of his bike and off they went for a spontaneous day out.

The Ashmolean was Britain's first public museum, with
some amazing treasures collected by Oxford's finest acade-
mics. Both Tanya and Harrison were intrigued by the history

of the original museum, which had combined its displays of rarities with the School of Natural history and a chemistry laboratory. Its founder, Elias Ashmole, had received his Doctorate in Medicine from the University and fourteen years later opened the museum in 1683.

The pair of them had spent hours wandering through the collection, marvelling at statues, Egyptian mummies and relics, prehistoric skulls and Roman artefacts. When they reached the *Princesses Fresco*, a painting from Egypt in around 1345 $_{BC}$, of the daughters of King Akhenaten, Tanya remarked on the shape of their elongated skulls.

'It's not hard to see why some people think the aliens built the pyramids when they depicted their royal families like that.'

'I believe it was just their style of art during this period, although there was also inbreeding because they were expected to marry within their own dynasty. That meant marrying siblings and the like.'

'No wonder they died young then.'

'This whole period when King Akhenaten ruled is interesting because he moved away from worshipping multiple traditional gods and instead worshipped one sun god. That probably added fire to the conspiracy theorists as it related to the sky where aliens might have first arrived from.'

'I can see why you get so interested in all this.' Tanya had smiled at Harrison.

He had been avidly looking at all the exhibits and reading every information card.

'Sorry, I guess I'm a bit geeky over all this stuff. Not the most exciting date. Are you getting bored?'

'I'm loving it,' she'd replied, 'your historical knowledge is amazing and, better still, you use it to solve crimes today.'

'It's the whole reason I set up the unit. Humans have been obsessed with the gods, spirits and ritual since the earliest times. Look at this carving, it's a supernatural spirit with the head of a raptor. The Egyptians did death and the afterlife like no one else and there will still be someone today who believes in at least some of what they believed in.'

'I find the sphinx and the crocodile and dog gods so creepy.'

'Anubis, he's the god with the jackal head. I think he's quite handsome, but yes, he was the god of the dead and supposed to lead souls into the afterlife. I think I'd have had nightmares when I was a kid if I'd expected to have to hold his hand after I'd died.'

Tanya had reached for Harrison's hand instead; warm life amid the mummies and ancient artefacts. He'd felt a contentment within himself that he'd never experienced, both enjoyable and frightening at the same time.

Since then, he'd been unable to see Tanya for a few nights due to work commitments, and he could almost hear the disappointment in her texts. He felt it too, but a part of him was also relieved because the more time he spent with her, the more he opened his heart – and he wasn't sure where that would lead. He really wasn't ideal boyfriend material, so judging Andrew was hardly fair.

Both of Andrew's parents were now dead, his mother only recently. She'd been forced to go into a care home after dementia had reduced her mobility and memory. Andrew spent four years watching her dignity and personality get taken from her, until she'd become a child in an old woman's body and he a stranger. He'd visited her every week, even when she'd no idea who he was. Last year she'd finally found release, and he'd buried her in the same plot as his father. Harrison had gone to the funeral to help him say goodbye.

Andrew was a Professor of Religions and Sacred Traditions at King's College, London. He'd joined the University when Harrison was in his first year of his psychology degree there, and they'd met in the library where Harrison had been indulging his favourite area of research, spiritualism and its impact on behaviours and the mind.

They had debated the question, *Is religion superstitious barbarism or spiritual enlightenment on our way to a greater purpose?*, with fervour, alternating sides. Andrew had guided Harrison to expand on the well-known positions of Freud and Jung, to consider all manner of ancient and modern theological and atheist theories, and the results and catalysts of both external and internal factors on the self. As Harrison's interest and knowledge grew, Andrew had introduced him to colleagues with expertise in Sanskrit and Ancient Greek culture, Franciscan thought, and Judaism. He had helped on research projects that compared modern-day cases of those who reported speaking with God and other spirits to the revered oracles of the old world whose revelations helped form the foundations of Christian and Ancient Greek and Hebrew society. Harrison had written a thesis questioning whether Moses, Abraham, Jesus and his followers would have been committed to psychiatric institutions by modern society, labelled as having psychotic or schizophrenic disorders, for saying they'd heard the voice of God or seen prophetic visions.

Andrew had also introduced him to the Harry Price Library at the University of London. It marked the start of years of research into the library's more than 13,000 documents relating to the paranormal, occult and magic, and a

lifelong obsession with man's need for spiritual enlightenment and how, when it went wrong, could result in murder
and crime.

Tonight, Harrison wanted to focus on his friend, rather
than their shared theological passions. The last time he'd
seen Andrew, he had seemed a little distracted – as though
something was preying on his mind. If Andrew needed help,
Harrison wanted to make sure he was available to be there
for him.

Harrison pulled up his Harley on the road outside
Andrew's house and, once parked, rang his friend's front
door. The familiar tring of the bell sounded inside the hallway, quickly followed by a light illuminating the stained-glass
window of the door, and Andrew's approaching footsteps.

Andrew appeared at the door. He was a big man; tall and
well-built, with the natural athletic physique of his
Caribbean heritage. It was only more recently, as Andrew's
hair had greyed around the edges, that Harrison had noticed
his paunch starting to expand. His shirt was crisp and
perfectly pressed. Andrew was always smartly dressed and
was rarely seen without a shirt and tie, but this evening, he'd
left his tie in its drawer.

'Harrison.' Andrew's face beamed at him, closely followed
by a warm hug. Harrison wasn't a man who usually did hugs,
but with Andrew he always made an exception. 'Looking
forward to some pasta tonight,' Andrew said. Half question,
half statement.

'Looking forward to the company more,' Harrison replied,
as he watched his friend punch in the code for the house
alarm. The keypad beeped at him, and he tried again, but got
the same result.

'Damned button keeps sticking,' he said to Harrison. 'Hang on while I get the panic alarm pad.'

Andrew quickly went into his study, where Harrison saw him reach into the top drawer of his desk and retrieve a small black keypad.

'Must get the alarm engineers out to fix that keypad,' he said as he returned to the hallway, punched in the numbers, and they both walked out the front door to the sound of the alarm setting itself.

Andrew climbed on the Harley behind Harrison, and they headed for Wimbledon, albeit with a little less acceleration capability than when he'd arrived.

Dinner was relaxed and enjoyable. A perfect combination of familiar surroundings, nice food, and good company. The restaurant owners fussed over Andrew, who they were on first-name terms with, betraying just how often he treated himself to his favourite food. Harrison suspected that was one reason Andrew's waistband was getting tighter; but in the grand scheme of things, it wasn't an issue. If you couldn't indulge yourself a little in your sixth decade, then when could you? As always when it came to alcohol, Harrison chose not to have his complimentary aperitif, and so Andrew had drunk both, before ordering a bottle of the Barolo for himself and some sparkling water for Harrison.

They talked about King's, the politics there, the latest research grants, and Harrison told him about the visit from Leo Fawcett.

'He's right, you know,' Andrew said, 'it's a feather in your cap. They wouldn't be chasing you if you weren't making a difference and getting results. It's a promotion and recognition of your work. It's what you wanted.'

'I guess,' Harrison had replied. He found it hard some-times to see the compliment in things.

Andrew's tongue had become looser as the meal went on, helped by the disappearing bottle of Barolo. Harrison saw no hint of the issue that had clearly been preying on Andrew's mind when they'd last met. Then Harrison told him about the meeting with Inspector Rob Morgan, and Andrew's mood changed. He told him what the police officer had said, and how Jack was looking into getting his mother's case reopened. Instead of what he'd expected to be an enthusiastic and empathetic response, when he finished speaking there was a stony silence.

Andrew wasn't looking at Harrison. He was staring grimly at the table in front of him. He took another large slug of wine.

'You may not like what I'm going to say now, but I have to say this to you. Do you not think it's time to move on and not stir up a hornets' nest?' Andrew looked up and stared into Harrison's eyes. His normally relaxed and friendly features were set, and his face seemed to have hardened into corners rather than its usual soft curves.

'What do you mean?'

'They're dangerous people, Harrison. You know they've killed twice, and it was all a long time ago now. Perhaps you should just focus on catching those who are threatening people today.' Andrew looked back down again, aware that his words would not have found a willing audience.

'You know how much this means to me. I've waited for this, for the moment when I could prove that they murdered my mother.'

'I know.' Andrew's voice had grown quiet. 'I just don't

want this to... I don't want it to consume you. I don't want to see you hurt.'

Harrison's stomach had tied itself into a knot. He felt anger and betrayal swirling around his insides. He couldn't believe what Andrew was suggesting.

'Hurt? How can they hurt me any more than they already have?'

Andrew stared straight at Harrison, determination and defiance replacing the friendly half-drunk warmth that had been in his eyes just minutes before.

'People like them will always find ways of hurting you.'

7

The moment he woke up the next morning, Harrison's mind went to the conversation with Andrew. The evening had ended a little awkwardly and although one conversation couldn't wreck a friendship that had lasted all his adult life, it had certainly left a bad taste in his mouth. Harrison had tried to work out why Andrew would have said what he did; he'd never intimated those thoughts before, and it was out of character. Andrew's default personality was positive and encouraging. It had been Andrew who'd given him the confidence to propose the setting up of the Ritualistic Behavioural Crime unit. As far as Harrison could tell, and he knew the man well, it hadn't been negative emotions behind Andrew's words. There was no anger, impatience, or even irritation. It wasn't that he was tired of Harrison talking about the subject. It had been concern Harrison had seen behind the frown on Andrew's face. So, what was Harrison missing?

With today being one of his twice-weekly fasting days, Harrison didn't need to worry about breakfast and was up and in the office early. Tanya was on his mind, so he texted her to see if she wanted to meet up later. Spending an evening with her would be a good antidote to the disappointment in his belly. He'd not seen her for a few days now, and he felt guilty that the last two evenings she'd proposed they meet up, he'd been busy. The first because it was the Tae Kwon Do night at the youth club. He didn't like to let the kids down, and there was one lad in particular that he'd wanted to connect with that evening. Yusuf had already been in trouble with the police, but he'd been trying hard to sort himself out. The last few weeks Harrison had noticed him wearing new trainers and clothes, and not only did he seem to be spending more time on his mobile phone, but he'd seen two phones in his possession. County lines drug dealers were always looking to recruit vulnerable young people to do their dirty work. If Harrison could help prevent one young life from being ruined, then he would. Unfortunately, Yusuf hadn't turned up. The first session he'd missed in eighteen months. Harrison had got in touch with his caseworker and shared his fears. He'd also called Yusuf's mother, but neither of them had been much help. It was no wonder the lad, and others like him, saw drug dealing as the only way to improve his circumstances, and his gang as the family to protect him.

Tanya texted back almost straight away with a sad emoji and the news she couldn't make tonight due to a departmental meeting. She suggested the following evening and Harrison gave the thumbs up. Thoughts of a pleasant few hours in her company cheered him up.

Harrison tried to concentrate on the emails which had already started stacking up in his inbox. They weren't just coming from Metropolitan police divisions, but from forces all over the UK. He had to admit that Leo Fawcett was right.

He was increasingly in demand all over the country and to stay under just one force's umbrella was wrong. It was time to have the conversation with Ryan.

Harrison's technical assistant didn't burst into the office with his usual enthusiasm. Ryan positively crept in.

'Boss,' he said to Harrison by way of greeting.

'Ryan, we need to have a chat about what Leo Fawcett proposed to me yesterday.'

Harrison saw the tremor of worry cross Ryan's face again.

'It's all positive. I'm really hoping you're going to be pleased,' he added quickly to reassure him.

'You mean they're not making me redundant?' Ryan's eyes squinted as he scanned Harrison's features for clues.

'Absolutely not. I need you. We are being promoted.' Harrison emphasised the 'we'.

It was like a pilot light had suddenly burst into life inside him. Ryan's whole demeanour changed from wilting lettuce to towering sunflower. If he'd been a dog, Harrison would have seen his ears prick up and tail wag energetically.

'I'll put the kettle on,' Ryan said, dumping his rucksack down beside his desk and heading over to their little sink in the corner. 'What's your poison? Mint or Chamomile?'

Repeating what Leo had said and explaining the situation to Ryan also helped Harrison to work through the situation in his own head.

'I think we should stay in London for the time being, until we're settled in to the NCA,' Harrison said to his assistant. Ryan had nodded eagerly. Harrison knew he suffered from agoraphobia. It wasn't just a case of being fearful of open spaces, it was more about unfamiliar environments. Ryan was comfortable with the daily journey from his flat to the office. Asking him to not only move office and job but also neighbourhood, all in one go, would put tremendous stress on him. No one else knew about his condition. They kept it between the two of them. Harrison wasn't about to expose him now.

'Do you think they'll get me a new computer?' he asked Harrison.

'I think we can pretty much ask for whatever it is we need.'

'I'll write up a spec now.' Ryan jumped up from the chair next to Harrison's desk where they'd been chatting.

'Thanks, Ryan.' Harrison smiled at him warmly.

'I hope they've got a decent canteen,' was all he replied. Normal business had been resumed.

Harrison returned to his emails. There was one from an officer in Streatham who was dealing with a churchyard vandalism incident. Someone had attempted to access a grave from the 1800s and they wanted to know if Harrison could explain why. He forwarded it to Ryan. This was just the kind of puzzle he liked to solve. Just as he pressed Send, his mobile rang.

DCI Sandra Barker's name flashed up.

'Sandra,' Harrison greeted her.

'Harrison, I need your help. Please.'

Sandra's voice conveyed the tension she was feeling.

'Of course,' he'd replied. It had to be serious for her to sound this stressed.

'It's Gemma,' she started. 'She says she's been confronted by a ghost, and a student has been murdered. I don't know what's going on, Harrison. Have you seen the newspapers? It's all over the nationals. Can you get to Durham and see what's happening? Detective Superintendent Adam Jackson has spoken to the chief constable there. They've not got any expertise for this kind of thing. Gemma isn't the only one.

About a hundred students have reported sightings, and locals too. It's getting out of control. They'd welcome your help, and so would I.'

Harrison went straight to the newspapers online to see what Sandra was referring to, and get a feel for what he might find.

The headlines ranged from 'Durham terrorised by murderous monk' and 'Is monk ghost prophesying disaster for Durham?' to 'Durham under Siege: Students fear for their lives'.

The newspapers said hundreds of students and locals had seen the ghost of a faceless monk walking the streets of the city in the past two weeks. Then, just two days ago, a student had been murdered, his body dressed in a monk's cloak and placed in a boat that was left to float down the River Wear. Police were baffled, and the University was trying to calm down students and parents who were threatening to leave in fear.

Harrison knew that most of the hype was going to be just that, hype, but there was clearly a problem. A student had been killed and from what Sandra said, although the police were unlikely to be totally 'baffled', they were struggling to understand what was going on.

'Ryan, your new tech spec will have to wait. I've got a job for you,' Harrison said. Five minutes later, he pressed Send on another text to Tanya. He had to blow her out yet again. He looked at Tanya's WhatsApp profile photo and sighed, before heading to his flat to pack a bag and fill up his bike with petrol ready for the four-and-a-half-hour journey north.

8

B y the time Harrison arrived in Durham, it was dark.
The city looked stunning with the cathedral and
castle illuminated. Harrison rode slowly across the
River Wear, its bridges lit up and shimmering in the water
below. He had the definite feeling of arriving in a city that
had been settled by people for centuries and was soaked in
their blood, troubles, and joy.

Ryan had put together a briefing document for Harrison
to give him some historical background on Durham –
monks were critical to the city's establishment and understanding the past could help in solving the current problem.
Harrison had never been before, but knew that despite its
small size, it was big on heritage and dramatic chronicles.
Durham Cathedral had been built over the last resting place
of Saint Cuthbert, a monk and hermit, who became a saint
after his death in AD 687. Cuthbert had briefly been the
Bishop of Lindisfarne, where his remains were originally
interred, but as the Danes looted the churches, the monks
carried his body to safety and he was eventually brought to

rest many years later in Durham in 995, when they effectively founded the city. The castle was built almost eighty
years later as an imposing fortress. Cuthbert's relic wasn't
alone, either. The head of Saint Oswald of Northumbria,
and the remains of The Venerable Bede, also lay in Durham
Cathedral.

The University was founded there in 1832, with the castle
designated its first college. It was still one of the top universi-
ties in the UK. There hadn't been any stories of monastic
hauntings in recent years, so whatever Harrison was travel-
ling to, it was something new. Ryan's research had given
Harrison the background to the city he needed, and Harrison
asked him to start monitoring social media and the student
chat boards for anything that related to their case. In the
meantime, he wanted to bring the history to life and experience the living city of today.

Despite itching to get started, Harrison was relieved to
reach the Radisson Blu. Riding the bike long distances was
always tiring, and he couldn't wait to get his leathers off and
have a good stretch and shower. It wasn't yet 7 p.m., and as he
didn't plan on eating until the morning, Harrison decided
he'd spend the evening wandering around the city before
bed. Stretch his legs after sitting on the bike.

He'd just placed his bag down in the room when his
phone went.

'Dr Lane? This is DS Urquhart, Major Crime team with
the Durham Constabulary. Welcome to the city. I'm going to
be your liaison. I understand you like to get stuck into a case
as soon as possible. Can I buy you dinner?'

'No dinner, thank you, but it would be good to meet up
and go through what you have so far and the major crime
sites.'

'Excellent. I'll meet you in the Radisson foyer at eight and give you a walking tour.'

DS DAVID URQUHART turned out to be a stick-thin Newcastle native in his mid to late twenties, with a penchant for burgers. He had just finished consuming a large one and had to go and wash his hands in the hotel bathroom before they could get underway.

'Sorry about that,' DS Urquhart said to Harrison when he re-joined him. 'I put too much ketchup on. Lucky it didn't go all over my Magpies jumper.'

The jumper in question was a black and white Newcastle United Football Club jumper, which was clearly a prized possession in David's wardrobe. Harrison thought it might have looked better with a good dollop of red ketchup. He wasn't singling out Newcastle, he just wasn't a football fan.

'I thought I'd show you the key areas for the ghost sightings – although to be honest they're coming in from all over now – and where we think the murder victim may have been placed in the boat,' DS Urquhart said. His accent was not as Geordie as some Harrison had met from the area; Harrison guessed he'd probably spent a fair amount of time away, which had smoothed some of the harder vowels.

'It's getting crazy out there. I've never seen anything like it. Since the murder, our Reception has been mobbed with people saying they've seen the ghost and we've had to put extra resource on the phones. So you do lots of this kind of thing then?' David immediately added. 'Those symbols on the victim's chest are freaky. I've never come across nowt like that before.'

'Symbols?'

'Yeah, on the murder victim, the monk. He had stuff carved into his chest. That's what we're hoping you're going to throw some light on.'

'Who was he?'

'A student, University College, which is in the castle. The family are very wealthy and well connected. We're looking at a host of potential motives. The mother is a hotshot financial lawyer, and the father is titled. Came from a long line of baronets or something like that. We need to cross the river.'

They had come out of the hotel, a modern building of mostly red brick and glass, and were immediately faced with a steel footbridge across the river. Harrison let DS Urquhart lead them across and within a minute or two, they were into the older part of the town where ancient brown stone buildings mingled with modern shop fronts. Arched windows and wooden doors sat next to glass panels advertising whatever treats lay within.

'That's the town hall over there,' DS Urquhart said. 'This is Silver Street which leads into Saddler Street and it's in that part of town that the ghost was originally seen. Down to our left is Elvet Bridge, which leads back across the river – that's where the two lads spotted the rowing boat with the victim in it.'

'I'd like to see where you think the murder took place first.'

'Well, we can't say for certain it did take place along the river. Obviously, he was put in a boat along here, but he could have been killed somewhere else entirely.'

'Of course.'

DS Urquhart looked at Harrison, trying to judge his reaction, and then continued. 'We've got two sites that the dog has shown an interest in, which would fit with the boat being launched, but no other evidence.'

They walked down and onto the path by the bank of the river.

'As you can see, there's not a great deal of space down here; it's just a narrow path with a wall and then the river. It's possible the murder took place further upstream. Not much further up there is the Hatfield College Boat Club, then Kingsgate Bridge.'

'Wasn't he from University College?'

'Yes, but their boat club is round the bend of the meander, so a fair way back upstream. We did send the dogs in, but they came back with nothing. The victim wasn't involved with the boat clubs. It's also a long way for it to have floated without somebody spotting it.'

'I thought it was late at night and dark.'

'It was, but it would have had to pass under Kingsgate Bridge and past quite a few buildings and restaurants which have a good view of the river. We've checked CCTV and nothing showed up.'

'Where does that path lead?' Harrison pointed to some railings on the top of the wall which led up through the undergrowth.

'Eventually takes you back out to Saddler Street again.'

'And the areas the dogs identified?'

'Here, where the wall is lower, and then further along where the path rises slightly. It would be easy to hide a boat in that undergrowth along the edge of the river there.'

'Risky to murder someone along a narrow path. How busy is this?'

Urquhart shrugged.

'We've asked potential witnesses to come forward, but

nothing so far. I wouldn't have thought at that time of night it was overly busy. Women would probably be put off by its remoteness and the tree and shrub coverage. Some couples might come along here, but at that time of night I'd say very few. He was spotted at gone 1 a.m.'

'Where was the boat from?'

'It was one of Browns' rowing boats. They're the other side of Elvet Bridge. We're trying to trace who hired their boats in the preceding forty-eight hours. At the moment we have one that we can't track down at all. Looks like a false name was given.'

'So, this was premeditated, or could the victim have already been dead?'

'He was only just dead when we got to him, so looks like there was planning involved.'

'Any other facts I should know?'

Urquhart thought for a moment. 'We have a theory that—'

Harrison held up his hand. 'Please, no theories, just facts right now.'

Urquhart shook his head. 'That's it on the boat then.'

HARRISON AND URQUHART left the relative darkness of the riverside and returned to Elvet Bridge and the city streets. The student population was evident everywhere. The narrow lanes were full of young people, some just walking, others chatting in groups. Harrison picked up snippets of conversations and heard the words 'monk' and 'ghost' mentioned more than once. This was clearly having a big effect on the city. In such an old and evocative place, it was easy to imagine how tales of those who had gone before could return and haunt the living. Small passageways between old buildings, unseeing statues of past heroes and the ever-present castle and cathedral looming over everything. In places like this, whispers and shadows could leach from walls and dark corners and easily infect vulnerable minds. Despite all this, Durham was a pretty city which reminded him in parts of a smaller version of Oxford, the streets tiled, or in some places, cobbled.

Urquhart stopped outside the Flat White cafe. 'The bulk of the ghost sightings are around here and the Palace Green area. They started about two weeks ago, but it's only since the murder that people have come forward to report them. We're getting about fifty students and locals come forward each day, and they are just the ones who come to us. We've seen more on social media.'

DS Urquhart was struggling to be heard above the sound of two men power-washing the wall of what looked like a modern red-brick addition, squeezed in between two older properties. They were trying to remove some graffiti from the wall. DS Urquhart and Harrison started walking again to get away from the noise.

'Hasn't the ghost been caught on CCTV?' Harrison asked.

'No, and that's also something we're struggling with,' the DS replied as they walked up the incline. 'We're getting a lot of sightings, but if it is someone playing a trick, or the killer, then they're clever and manage to avoid cameras in the city. They also just seem to disappear. Some people have reported following the ghost and they seem to vanish into thin air. All we've had is the odd potential glimpse on CCTV, but we're not even sure it is the ghost... This is Owengate which leads to Palace Green.'

Durham's vast cathedral came into full view, its stone

tower rising above the surrounding buildings. There was no doubting it all looked impressive.

'I thought the ghost had attacked some girls too?'

'Well, attacked is probably too strong a word. One girl received a scratch to her face from the rose. She was the first to report it – she saw him before the murder.'

'The rose?'

'Yes, the ghost sometimes carries a single red rose stem, just like the one found with the body in the boat. One of the girls who saw the ghost got a bit cocky; she'd been drinking, and so tried to take the ghost's cowl off its head. She got swiped in the face and the rose must have had a thorn. When her friends tried to chase the ghost, it just disappeared into thin air.'

'Interesting,' said Harrison. 'Is there a set route it takes?'

'Other than the majority of sightings around the cathedral area, no. We've had extra officers out, but so far nothing. We've mapped it all; the boss should have got it all emailed over to you by now.'

'OK, and anything else?'

'Not really. At the moment we don't know how the victim got to the boat, whether he was killed at the riverside or somewhere else, and other than the obvious – that the ghost is also a monk – we don't know what the connection is between the two. We have assumed there's a connection as they are both in monk's clothing.'

They stood for a few moments on the Green. DS Urquhart had run out of information and was weighing up what to say next.

'OK, well thank you for the tour, DS Urquhart. If you don't mind, I'll have a wander around on my own now and see you in the morning.'

The DS looked taken aback. 'That it? You don't want me to stick around and guide you back to your hotel?'

'No, thank you. I can assure you I've memorised the route. I find it useful just to take in the atmosphere of a place and concentrate.' Harrison held his hand out to the stunned DS with the aim of ending the conversation. 'I appreciate your time.'

'OK, right. Good night.' The DS looked at his watch. 'If you do fancy a drink, I'll be in The Court Inn with a couple of the lads. You're welcome to join us.'

Harrison tipped his head in thanks and watched as DS Urquhart turned and walked the way they'd just come, with just one curious backward glance at him.

Harrison sat down on a wooden bench in Palace Green, just in front of a flower bed filled with rose bushes that had finished their blooms for the year and were preparing to hunker down for the cold winter. He needed to hunker down too and immerse himself in this small city.

It felt totally different to London – a microcosm of its own, thousands of students and academic staff from around the world packed into a northern city steeped in tradition and history. Add to that a good dose of tourists, and the local people and character were combined into a multicultural soup of humanity. Somehow, though, the traditions and history were the blueprint on which all this life existed. It was like a sandcastle bucket. It didn't matter what kind of sand you put into it, the grains followed the same grooves and the shape was always the same at the end.

Sitting on the bench now, surrounded by Durham Castle and Cathedral, he could feel the history seeping out from the stone walls of the buildings and the ground beneath him. Mature trees were scattered throughout the city and clustered the riverbanks. There was no doubting the beauty of the place, or its heritage, but somewhere, there was an evil element. A grain of black sand that had got into the bucket with its golden counterparts and was making the castle crumble at the edge. Who was the culprit and why they were here, he didn't yet know, but the marks on the victim's chest were going to be his starting point.

9

Harrison was at the morgue by 9:30 a.m., the earliest appointment the pathologist could give him. The ride up yesterday had tired him out and given him an appetite, so when morning came, he'd treated himself to a full English breakfast at the hotel to break his fast. It was only when he'd arrived at the morgue and was waiting for the pathologist to take him through, that he wondered if the greasy breakfast had been a wise move. He had ten minutes to contemplate that question before it would be answered.

The pathologist, Sunil Sharma, turned out to be a tall, shiny-headed man who Harrison soon learned, had been brought up in Uttar Pradesh in India. His smile was warm and honest, and Harrison knew instantly that Sunil was someone who would do his absolute best for every one of his clients. Harrison followed him through the featureless grey corridors to his office, where he found a riot of colour and cheerfulness which radiated the character of its host. Harrison knew he wouldn't have been the first person to wonder how the pathologist could be so positive about life when faced with death every working day. He suspected it had a lot to do with mindset and perhaps the statue of the Hindu god, Vishnu, on the desk was an indicator. Vishnu, the preserver and protector, restores the balance of good and evil in the world. Sunil was regularly faced with the results of evil, but he worked hard to restore the balance of justice and give the victims a voice.

Judging by the mounted certificates on the office wall, education was also important to Sunil and a source of pride.

The office also had a warm smell of ginger and spices – a vast improvement on what would greet them in the examination rooms.

'Tea? It's ginger chai – or I can get you something else like PG Tips or coffee?' Sunil picked up his own mug from his desk and walked over to a side table where a warming plate held a large metal teapot.

Harrison rarely had caffeinated drinks, but the chai smelt delicious, and he could imagine its warmth in his stomach. 'A small one, thank you,' he replied, hearing the adage *when in Rome* in his head.

'I make it myself, fresh ginger and cardamom, plus some family spices, and of course a little sugar,' Sunil said, and handed over a half-filled mug of steaming milky tea which smelled delicious. 'Plenty more if you like it.'

'Thank you. I don't usually drink caffeinated tea or coffee so I'll go easy.' Harrison took a sip and felt its warmth slide down his throat. 'It's good.'

Sunil nodded and smiled. 'Sets my constitution up for the day. Now, let us look at our young man.'

The young man in question was George Rupert Harold Marshwood, a twenty-year-old law student at the university, who had been in line to inherit the title of Baron Marshwood from his father. It was a minor title, but his father had been a stockbroker at the height of the financial boom in the eighties, and his mother commanded high rates as a lawyer, so he would have also got a share in a fairly large inheritance. His younger brother, Charles, would now benefit from the lot. All this Sunil read out to Harrison from the information on his screen. Harrison could tell he didn't care about whether the corpse in his mortuary cold room had a title and money, simply that he was a human being who had been murdered and deserved justice.

Next, Sunil turned his screen around so that Harrison could see the images he brought up from George Marshwood's file.

'These will give you a clear view of the markings on his torso, because obviously I have had to make incisions for the examination. He was poisoned. Death would have been fairly quick, but brutal. You notice the way his face has contorted? He would have had paralysed facial muscles, low blood pressure, and then slow paralysis of the heart. It was Monkshood, a common plant, sometimes called Wolfbane or aconite.'

'Yes, I've come across it before,' said Harrison.

'We believe the killer boiled up leaves and roots of the plant and put it into an alcoholic drink. A mix of vodka, apple and orange juice, honey and rum. There were high concentrations of the aconite so there's no doubting the intention.'

Sunil indicated the three symbols carved into the skin of George Marshwood's torso, which seemed to have been made hurriedly. 'They inflicted the wounds as he was dying, before death. He is likely to have been just alive when placed in the boat. He had not been gone long when they found him.'

Harrison examined the photographs of George's skin. The

dominant feature was what looked like an upside-down hangman's cross, but with the cross bar bent downwards at the ends. Underneath this, across his stomach, were the letters *i u s t i t i a.*

'Justice. This is some kind of revenge killing,' Harrison thought out loud. 'The symbol is the Satanic justice symbol, and the letters are justice in Latin.'

'We got the Latin quite early on, but the other symbol we were not sure about. There is something else too: a small tattoo, placed discreetly on his left hip bone.'

Sunil clicked through the photographs and came to what looked like a capital *M* with a small *u* and a teardrop shape dripping from it. They'd been created in black ink and stood out clearly against the victim's marble white skin.

'*Mu*? No idea on that one,' said Sunil.

'If you follow the pattern of the carvings, then that could be the Greek letters, capital M and a lowercase m.' Harrison said.

'As you can see, it is homemade. Either George, or someone else has cut into his skin and then put ink into the wound to create the tattoo. I don't think it is likely to have been George: if you look at the position and angle, he would have had to use a mirror and you know how difficult that is when you are looking at something in reverse. I do not think this was self-inflicted. It is also a fairly painful, and barbaric, way of having a tattoo done. Small needles are bad enough, but this involved slicing his flesh. Bearing in mind the nature of the symbols on his chest and how they were created, it is a similar process.'

'How old would you say the tattoo is?'

'Maybe as much as two years, I would say. The parents did not realise he had it.'

'Anything else unusual about him?'

'Yes. One final oddity. There was a small, triangular-shaped piece of skin cut from his upper buttock around the time of death. Neatly done. Presumably at the same time his killer was carving up his chest.'

'A trophy, maybe?'

'Perhaps. That is your department. All I can say with certainty is that it was removed.'

'What about any signs of a struggle?'

'Nothing that would indicate a fight of any form. There was some debris under his nails, which looked like they had been scraped across a hard surface and mud, but I am thinking that was probably inflicted when he was dying in agony from the poison. There was some dust on his knees so he likely collapsed onto the ground, and some bruising where he was hoisted into the rowing boat. That is it.'

'Ever seen anything like this through here before?'

Sunil shook his head and took a big sip of his chai. 'Do you want to go and see him now?'

If Harrison was honest, he could do without it. The body had been completely examined and a full post-mortem undertaken. It was therefore highly unlikely that he would be able to glean any extra clues from it. Ideally, he'd have seen it in situ, prior to Sunil getting his hands on George, but that couldn't have been helped.

'I'll take a quick look, just to make sure I have those markings and the tattoo clear in my head.'

Harrison wasn't squeamish about death. He didn't see a cadaver as a person. They were empty husks the moment death took them. He'd felt that way ever since he'd gone to see his mother in the mortuary. As next of kin, he'd been asked to identify her, and he'd also needed to see her for his own closure.

He'd been at his grandmother's deathbed not long after. Seeing someone just after they had passed away was the closest he'd ever got to believing in the spirit as its own separate entity. She'd been there, the warmth of her personality and experience filling her cancer-wracked body and then, with her last breath, she was gone. He could understand why some societies believed in opening windows to let the spirit out and free.

In some ways, not seeing the victim's bodies as people helped him to deal with the gruesome sights he had to see, and the cruelty inflicted by others. He could view them as another clue in the case. At the same time, connecting to their past lives and remembering that they were once living, breathing human beings was part of his job. He also always made the same silent promise to every one of them – as he did now to George Marshwood – that he would find his killer and make sure nobody else had to join him.

10

Harrison's next stop was the incident room to look through all the evidence and the state of the inquiry. He also needed to see DCI Sandra Barker's daughter Gemma for her mother, but the case – and getting a full grounding into what was going on – came first.

The Major Crime Team were based at the Chester-le-Street police station. The fifteen-minute drive from Durham towards Newcastle was easy, taking Harrison along open roads lined by trees before arriving in the old market town. The police station was an uninspiring modern, brown squat building in a residential area.

Harrison's arrival into the incident room was perfectly timed. While there seemed to be a distinct lack of bums on seats in the main office, he saw a group, including DS Urquhart, in a meeting room. Harrison saw DS Urquhart spotted him straight away, said something to the man at the head of the table, and then jumped up and out of the room to greet Harrison.

'Dr Lane, we've just started the prayer meeting. Come on in.'

Harrison looked at him, a little nonplussed.

'Morning briefing,' David explained and waved him forward.

Harrison walked into the meeting room and all eyes turned to look at the tall, muscular man in black bike leathers.

'Dr Lane, glad you could join us.' The man at the head of the table stood up and walked along the side to shake his hand. 'DI John Steadman, Senior Investigating Officer.' DI Steadman was a tall, big-boned man with jet-black hair and a hint of a suntan to his skin which was out of place in the chilly north of England and made Harrison think he was probably of Italian or Mediterranean descent. He looked like he had once been a fan of the gym, but the extra work of being a DI, and the longer hours sat on his backside, had softened his contours. The crucial point for Harrison was his welcoming smile, which spread across his entire face. The reception here was distinctly warmer than the last one he'd received in Norfolk. They seemed genuinely pleased to see Harrison. It would make for a significantly more pleasant visit. Although even if things were frostier, he'd have just got on with it anyway.

Harrison shook hands with DI John Steadman.

'As I mentioned yesterday, Dr Harrison Lane is head of the Met's Ritualistic and Behavioural Crime unit,' he addressed the room, 'and we are lucky that he has agreed to assist us on this case. He has full clearances and I expect you to give your full cooperation. Dr Lane—'

'Harrison, please,' he interjected.

The DI nodded. 'Harrison, we were just about to have a

catch-up, so it's good that you can have a listen in, and then I'm sure the team will have some questions, as will you. Take a seat.' He waved towards the empty chairs and Harrison walked round the table to a spare place next to a uniformed petite twenty-something redhead with freckles dotted across her face. She shifted in her seat as he sat down and Harrison wondered if he'd embarrassed or intimidated her. He hoped neither. DS Urquhart winked and smiled at the young woman in a gesture of support. A moment later, Harrison heard her let out the breath she'd been holding.

'OK people,' DI Steadman began. 'For the benefit of Dr— Harrison, I'll do a full recap. The deceased, George Marshwood, was spotted floating down the Weir in a rowing boat, in the early hours of Tuesday morning. Two lads standing on Elvet Bridge had seen the boat and alerted two PCs. When the boat was retrieved, George had been dead less than an hour. The post-mortem showed he had been poisoned. George was dressed in a monk's cloak and found clasping a single red rose.

Investigations have centred on the family and the students who lived with George. There are five of them in the house, but there's no obvious motive as to why they would poison him, and they all claim to not be involved and have given each other alibis. We have also been looking for the murder site. So far we have no motive, no clear suspects, and no evidence other than George himself.' DI Steadman let out a deep, involuntary sigh. 'If it wasn't for the chest carvings, I'd wonder if it was murder at all and instead suicide or an accident, but I'm assuming, Harrison, that you would agree the marks point to intention to kill?'

'Yes, definitely. I believe you already know that the Latin

word on his chest means justice, and the symbol is a Satanic justice symbol. Both point to this being a revenge killing.'

Steadman nodded and continued, 'I also don't see why a law student would boil up poisonous flowers to make a drink. There are easier ways of ending your life. The fact they used Monkshood is another link to the obvious theme that's going on here. Revenge could point to somebody that the mother has either defended or sent down. She's a lawyer, so I need someone to take a close look at that angle for us, especially if there are any cases relating to the church. Did she perhaps defend a member of the clergy accused of abuse? Been a fair few of those trials in the last few years.'

A young detective spoke up: 'Sir, we found nothing at George's student house to link with the creation of the poison.'

'No, but I still have my suspicions about that lot. They know more than they're letting on. Harrison, you should look at their statements. The housemates' stories are all too rehearsed, plus they came fully lawyered-up. All from wealthy families who have already started applying pressure on us to keep away from their boys. It's beyond co-witness convergence. My money is their briefs have them all working from the same script.'

'Or they might be scared and have created a story to protect themselves,' added Harrison.

'Scared of being caught?'

'No. Scared of whoever killed George. This was a clear public statement. If the killer had just wanted him dead, he would have poisoned him and been done with it. There's theatrics in the way he was found. They wanted to send a clear message to somebody.'

'Any thoughts on the tattoo?' The DI asked Harrison.

He shook his head. 'It could be anything at this stage. I'm guessing it's the Greek letters Mm.'

'A girlfriend's initials, maybe?' Steadman asked.

'It would be strange to put a girlfriend's initials into Greek. That's usually reserved for secret societies. It's quite common for them to have a two- or three-word motto or name.'

'You saying George could have been part of some kind of Satanic cult?'

'I'm saying there's a possibility that George was part of some kind of secret society which either believes he has betrayed them, or is under attack from someone else who is sending a message to the group.'

'We need to see if any of his housemates have that tattoo,' John said to the room.

'What about the ghost?' Harrison questioned.

'Ah yes, the ghost. The bane of all our lives. Every news organisation under the sun seems to be obsessed with the ghost and he's taking up an inordinate amount of our resources. Sightings started being reported on social media, but we put it down to students having a laugh. It escalated after the murder. Lucy, you've been collating all that.' The DI addressed the petite redhead next to Harrison, who immediately turned the colour of the red rose George had been holding.

'Yes. We've had just over a hundred reported sightings so far. About half are around the Sadler Street and Palace Green area. They all involve seeing a monk with no face in a black cloak, and often he's carrying a single red rose.'

'We're obviously linking this to our inquiry due to the monk and rose connection,' DI Steadman explained, unnecessarily. 'The so-called ghost was seen before the murder, although not reported until after it.'

'And since?' Harrison asked.

'Yes. So it couldn't have been George.'

'Initially, most of the witnesses weren't bothered by it. They thought it was a publicity stunt or a student in fancy dress. It's only since George was killed that they've started calling him a ghost and coming to us. It's a bit odd that they all say he has no face...' Lucy said. She avoided eye contact with Harrison, but had slightly angled herself towards him. 'We can't find any evidence of him on CCTV, and he appears to disappear into thin air, which is fuelling the paranormal theory.'

'Have you attached any significance to the rose yet?' Harrison asked.

They shook their heads.

'Only thing we can think of is the War of the Roses back in the fifteenth century. The red rose was the symbol of the House of Lancaster, who were up against the Yorks. But that's a tentative link which doesn't seem to have anything to do with George's family or their title.'

Harrison nodded. 'Any indications as to why a monk?'

'Durham was founded by monks, and the body of Saint Cuthbert is buried at the cathedral. He was a monk, and that's where most of the sightings have been,' Lucy replied.

'One female student sustained a deep scratch to her face after trying to confront the ghost. Several others have since reported that the monk tried to attack them and a few say they are being haunted by him. You're going to be better placed than us in interviewing them and getting to the bottom of their stories,' DI Steadman said to Harrison. 'We are trying to track this ghost down. He could obviously be our killer.'

'What about any other unexplained crimes in the run up to the murder?' Harrison asked.

DI Steadman pulled his mouth down and his shoulders up. 'Nothing that's come to our attention. What kind of things are you thinking about?'

'Difficult to say, but just things that are out of the ordinary, never solved. Perhaps missing or mutilated pets or strange graffiti?'

'Anybody?' Steadman asked the room.

They all shook their heads and looked at Harrison.

'We're Major Crime so the small stuff's not really on our radar. We can get you access to the full database and perhaps you might spot something significant?'

'That will be fine.' Harrison knew just the man for that job.

'Any other questions?' Steadman asked him.

'Not a question, but you are all referring to the killer as *him*. Poisoning is often a woman's choice of murder weapon. The justice could be referring to a lover's tiff. I'll develop a profile as soon as I can, but you need to keep your mind open with regards gender.'

'We figured more likely male as they had to lift him into the boat,' Steadman replied.

'Maybe, maybe not. From what you say, he might not have been dead and could have got himself into the boat. Maybe been tricked, or thought he was getting away. At this stage I'd remain open-minded.'

'Fair enough. Good point, Dr Lane. Steve, can you double-check George's love life again for us?' He addressed a young

Black officer, who nodded in response. Harrison looked around the table. The team looked like a cohesive and diverse bunch with a healthy respect for John. That was important. Harrison had worked with teams that were made up of trusted faces who were invariably a reflection of the person leading them. Those teams were never as effective as one chosen for their skills, and with a good mix of diversity. Coming at a case with just one main viewpoint and experience was never going to let you see the whole picture. Plus, all too often, a team's respect was begrudging or earned out of fear. From what he'd seen of John so far, Steadman was open to listening. There'd been many an SIO in the past few years who had closed his ears to Harrison's opinions and suggestions and regretted it.

The meeting broke up with a scraping of chairs, but Harrison could tell morale was already dipping. They weren't making progress, and that was never good this early in an investigation.

The first thing Harrison did was set Ryan on the case.

'I need you to search all the crime reports for the area, and also social media and the usual places for anything which is out of the ordinary in the last eighteen months. You know the kind of thing I'm talking about. Plus, do a thorough background search on George Marshwood and his family. Apart from the usual potential enemies, are there any links to secret societies in their past or present? I'm also looking for a society that has the initials of two M's. Are there any secret societies active around Durham? I know Oxford and Cambridge have secret societies among University students, perhaps it's the same here. I'll send you over a list of the housemates' names. We need to do thorough checks on them too.'

'OK, boss,' Ryan replied. 'There's a ton of stuff coming up on the student chat boards as well. Most of it is about the ghost, or just gossip. I suppose you need this all yesterday?'

'As soon as you can, Ryan. I don't want to see another body.'

Harrison knew Ryan would work all hours to get him the information. He could rely on Ryan, but Harrison had given him a lot to do and it would take time. Around 64,000 crimes were reported to Durham Constabulary in a year, and while Ryan wouldn't be trawling through each one individually – he had his own programmes and algorithms for spotting those that would interest them – that alone would inevitably take some time.

Harrison's priority was the ghost. While it was clear that DI Steadman and his team felt the ghost monk might be their killer, Harrison knew that the key to catching them was going to be working out their agenda and motivation. He needed to start by looking through the statements and report logs of all the sightings. He'd also need to speak to some of the witnesses himself. But first, he had to sort out the chaff from the wheat. Who had seen the monk and where, and if there was any underlying pattern to their reports.

The young female detective who'd sat next to Harrison in the briefing plucked up the courage to introduce herself and show him how to access all the statements. DC Lucy Armstrong was efficient and thorough.

'These are all from the last forty-eight hours, apart from the girl who got scratched,' he said to her.

'Yes, none of them reported the ghost to us until after George's murder,' she replied. 'They were talking about it online and amongst themselves, but it wasn't really a police matter apart from the assault and then the link to the murder.'

'But the ghost was definitely seen before his death?' Harrison queried.

'Yes, but they didn't think it was overly unusual until George was found. As soon as a couple of people came forward, it opened the floodgates.'

Harrison thought for a few moments. He could feel Lucy watching him intently.

'Is everything OK?' she asked him, not used to his periods of quiet.

'Yes, fine. So what timeframes are we talking between the event and reporting it?'

'Up to two weeks. You're thinking their statements are going to be inaccurate, aren't you?'

'We know that witnesses are unreliable at the best of times. No reflection on the individuals, it's just fact. You add in the length of time between the initial incident, and then the various influences from social media, stories heard in bars and from friends, and those memories are going to be quite severely tainted. I would guess that most of the statements are very similar?'

Lucy nodded and looked disappointed.

'Did you take all the statements?'

'Yes.'

'What questions did you ask them?'

'How we've been trained, I let them tell me what happened in their own words first, and then I sought to clarify points.'

'And how did you refer to the individual they'd seen?'

'I don't know what you mean?'

'During the interviews, was the monk referred to as a ghost or as a person?'

'Well, at first we thought it was George. We had a body in a monk's cloak and then people coming forward saying they'd seen someone wandering around dressed as a monk. We hoped it might give us some ideas about what George had been doing before his murder. Then we got reports of people seeing him after George had been found and I suppose those witnesses tended to use the term ghost more often, and that's when we questioned if it was the same person after all. I referred to him as just "the monk" in my questions.'

'OK, thank you for your help,' Harrison said to Lucy and began to look through the reports on the screen in front of him.

'I can show you the ones which came across to me as being the most interesting,' Lucy suggested.

'No, thank you. I'd like to read through them myself,' Harrison replied. Lucy would have brought her own subjectivity to the interviews. He needed to look at them with a fresh eye and as much objectivity as he could. She looked a little upset at his words, but Harrison needed to focus. He was already zoning out the office noise around him and channelling his concentration. Eventually, Lucy wandered off back to her own desk, but he was aware of her eyes on him from across the incident room.

Half an hour later, she reappeared at his desk. 'Can I get you a coffee?' she asked, peering at the screen.

'No, thank you.' He smiled at her, putting it down to eagerness rather than being nosey.

. . .

BY LUNCHTIME, Harrison had read all the statements from the five housemates: Oscar, Joseph, James, Mark and David. They made for interesting reading, not because of anything they said, but more in the way they said it. DI Steadman had intimated as much to him in the briefing, and Harrison agreed – at least in part. All five statements were indeed virtually identical. They recounted the same story of the day that George was killed. Harrison was also sure their statements were rehearsed, but he didn't agree that it was the lawyers who had set them up to do it. The language was wrong. There were a few identical comments which were distinctly amateurish, and a complete lack of legal speak which he would have expected had they rehearsed the statements with lawyers.

Without a doubt there was some kind of conspiracy, but the question was whether it was born out of fear, or because they were hiding a murder. He'd read statements like this before, where several people had colluded to ensure they told the same story in order to ensure they didn't slip up after being threatened by a third party. Were George's housemates in danger too, or were they hiding something?

SHORTLY AFTER LUNCH, DI Steadman came to find Harrison. The detective rubbed at the dark shadows under his eyes.

'How's it going, Harrison?'

'Fine.' By this point, Harrison was glad of the interruption. He'd been staring at the screen for hours, reading and cross-checking, and he needed a screen break.

'We drew a blank on girlfriends for George. He didn't seem to have any particular female friend that we can tell. Looked through his phone photos too and they seem to back that up.'

'What about the friends in the house, any luck with seeing if they have the tattoo?'

Steadman hmphed. 'Nope, brick wall from the parents and lawyers. Invasion of privacy, no charges brought, they're not suspects etc. etc. It's a no-go right now unless we can get something more concrete on them.'

Harrison wasn't overly surprised.

'DS Urquhart contacted George's parents,' John continued, 'asked them if their son might have been part of a secret association. They kindly said they would arrange for him to be relieved of his house and all other earthly possessions if he considered damaging their son and family's reputations in public. They're lawyered to the hilt. We're having to tread on eggshells with this one. The parents won't allow a word said against their precious offspring.'

'I'll be careful, don't worry,' Harrison replied, and he had every intention of trying.

11

While he waited for Ryan to turn up some information, Harrison decided to start visiting some of the students who'd reported sightings of the ghostly monk. He was becoming convinced that the 'ghost' was the key to all this. He'd been seen prior to George being killed, as well as after. It was obviously linked somehow – he just needed to figure out how. He'd read through all the sighting reports, and some clear patterns had formed. Two witnesses in particular seemed to give more detail and also were from before George's murder, after which many of the reports became almost identical.

His first visit was with an Alice Robertson, who was their first-known sighting. She'd seen the monk before the girl was assaulted with the rose. Alice was a student at University College: the same college as the victim George Marshwood. Harrison had arranged to rendezvous at the top of Owengate by the red public telephone box – an unusual sight in these days of mobile phones – on the edge of Palace Green.

It was a pleasant early evening, although there was a chill

to the air. Harrison could tell he was further north. Up here they still had regular snow falls, unlike the warmer south, which rarely saw the white stuff. He had dropped by the hotel to leave his bike and freshen up, and was now grateful for the jumper he'd brought with him. He walked briskly to warm up.

The streets had thinned out of the general public as the shops were now shut; there were mostly just students milling about now, or a few tourists out for an early meal.

Harrison loved the feel of this little city. In fact, it didn't feel like a city at all. Not like London with its incessant traffic, teeming streets and constant hubbub. It turned his mind to Leo Fawcett's offer. Maybe it was time for him to move out of London. He had never intended to stay – the city life had never suited him. He'd stayed because he was lucky to have a home, thanks to his grandfather's inheritance, and because his dear friend Andrew was there. Then he'd set up the unit and met Ryan, and so he'd ended up staying longer. What would he be leaving behind if he left now? Apart from Andrew's face, one other came into his mind. Tanya. Although they didn't see each other too regularly, he'd definitely miss her company. She'd texted earlier to see how it was going. She was out tonight, but perhaps he'd get to speak to her if she didn't get home too late.

Alice Robertson turned out to be a bright, bubbly young woman from Bedford with long curly brown hair. She came with backup: a girl from Manchester called Kaz, with a personality double her size and a mass of African-Caribbean hair. The two girls appraised Harrison.

'I told Kaz about it, didn't I?' Alice explained, and her friend nodded energetically. 'Thought it was right weird cos I couldn't see their face, but you just never know if it's someone from the cathedral or another student having a laugh. I didn't bother telling the police until after the murder.'

'Can you think back to that night and tell me where you were and what time it was?' Harrison asked her.

'I'd just come out the Castle, been in the Undie and it was about half nine-ish,' she replied, and then saw Harrison's quizzical look.

'The Undercroft: it's our college bar. I hadn't drunk much, just a couple. I don't drink a lot, do I Kaz?'

'No, she doesn't drink much, don't like getting drunk, do you?'

'So it was dark, and I started heading towards my room when I saw this black figure walking along the side of Palace Green. Over there.' She pointed further along the side of the Green that they were now on.

'Did you see where they had come from?'

Alice shook her head.

'They walked over to that garden bit over there and laid down the rose they were carrying, stood there a few moments and then walked off towards the cathedral. When I looked again, they'd just disappeared.'

Harrison looked to where Alice had pointed out the flower bed. It was close to where he'd sat on the bench just yesterday looking at the rose bushes. It was a patch of around twelve feet by six feet.

'And did the monk seem real to you?'

'I thought so, but their footsteps never made any sound. I only realised after. They were light on their feet and they didn't have a face under the hood. It was just black inside.'

Harrison smiled and nodded.

'I promise you I saw him, but he didn't attack me or anything, like some people say. Didn't really seem to bother about me at all. I thought that was a bit odd, too. They say some hauntings are like film clips that keep replaying? That they're printed on old buildings and stuff?'

'Some people believe that. It's more likely that it was a person dressed as a monk,' Harrison replied.

'But I definitely didn't see a face.'

'They were probably wearing a black face mask in case they were recognised.'

'They did just disappear,' Alice argued.

'Were you standing still watching them?'

'No, I was walking back home.'

'Then chances are you would have glanced away more than once to check your footing or to look where you were going. In those few seconds, someone could go into a building or down a side street and disappear from your view.'

'So you don't believe the monk's a ghost then?' Kaz asked, genuinely interested.

'Our brains will interpret things according to circumstances, and our memories change over time. It's not like extracting a piece of data from a computer; a memory can be altered just by telling someone. Did you think you'd seen a ghost when you first told Kaz?' Harrison asked Alice.

She thought a moment, shrugged her shoulders, and then shook her head.

'It's because of all the rumours and the murder that you are questioning what it was you witnessed. Making the memory fit the current circumstances.'

'I'm not lying...' She pouted.

'No, I'm not saying you are. I believe what you saw that night; it's just a question of interpretation. Your brain now has other information in relation to that incident, so it's imposing different criteria onto what it was you saw.'

Alice thought about it and nodded. 'Yeah, I can see that,' she said.

'Not such a great story to tell in the Undie though.' Kaz laughed. 'Definitely better when it was a murdering ghost.'

The two girls headed off giggling and left Harrison thinking. There was one other student to speak to before he headed off to find some dinner. Josh Findley was a student at Trevelyan College, one of the hill colleges further out of the main city area. Josh had also agreed to meet Harrison at the Green and he guessed that the skinny, bookish-looking lad that had just arrived at the phone box was him.

'Josh?' Harrison asked.

Josh visibly jumped at Harrison, and his eyes widened as he took him in.

'Harrison Lane, we spoke on the phone.'

'Yes, yes, that's me,' he replied. 'You're the psychologist?' he asked, surprised, giving Harrison a quick look over. He spoke fast, reminding Harrison of a chattering sparrow.

'I won't keep you long. I wanted to get an idea of what it was you saw. Can you think back to that night?'

'I told the police. I was coming across the Green, you know, just been to see a friend, and I saw him walking across from there,' Josh pointed towards Owengate, 'and over to there.' He indicated the flower bed again. 'Then he went off down past the Department of Music, towards the river.'

'Where's that?'

'Next to the cathedral.'

'What time was this?'

'About half past midnight. I'd been with my friend, you know, working on a project with him,' Josh qualified. 'He's on the same course as me.'

Harrison smiled at him reassuringly. It was obvious that

Josh hadn't yet come to terms with his own sexuality and felt the need to cover his tracks.

'Did they do anything? The monk?' Harrison asked.

'Just stopped over there for a bit. I wasn't watching all the time.' Josh pointed to the flower bed again. 'It was before that guy was murdered and I thought it was just someone coming back from a party.'

'So you thought it was a real person?'

'I thought so, yes. They seemed real enough.'

'Anything about the monk that stood out to you?'

'I couldn't see their face – I suppose that's a bit odd. Under the hood was just dark.'

'What kind of size were they?'

'Not as tall as me, but slim.'

Harrison estimated that Josh was about five feet eleven. 'So they just walked down the side of the cathedral. You didn't see exactly where they went?' he asked.

'No, I wanted to get home. It was late. Like I said, I didn't think anything of it.'

'OK, thank you, Josh. I appreciate your time.'

Josh couldn't seem to get away fast enough, and half ran and half walked across the Green towards the Castle entrance in the far right-hand corner. No doubt off to visit his friend again.

Harrison stopped a moment and considered what Alice and Josh had both said. The mysterious monk had walked up Owengate and along the side of Palace Green, stopping at the flower bed, before disappearing down towards the river. He'd done the same thing both times. There were a couple of other eyewitnesses who mentioned the monk walking the same route. But why was the flower bed so important?

Harrison walked over to take a closer look. It was full of

rose bushes, none of them in bloom, of course, due to the time of year. Why would someone dressed in a monk's robe place a rose amid rose bushes? Harrison looked around Palace Green. This was getting interesting, but what it all meant, he didn't yet know.

12

W hen Harrison got back to his hotel room, the first thing he did was call Tanya. He told himself it was because he felt guilty for having let her down, but if he was honest, it was because he missed her company and her voice. He'd tried to reason with himself, to quell the tension he felt every time he thought about getting more involved with her, but it wouldn't go away. Something inside of his head, something hidden, was blocking his ability to fully commit. He missed her, he wanted her, but he just couldn't do it. Psychoanalysing himself wasn't working out, but he wouldn't give up trying.

Tanya answered, and Harrison could hear she was in a car or taxi.

'Harrison, I'm just on my way home,' she said.

'OK, did you have a good night?'

'What did you say?'

'Did you have a good night?'

'Oh yes, thank you. It was lovely, actually. Look, I can

barely hear you. Give me a call a bit later, can you? If you're going to bed, don't worry, I'll call you in the morning.'

'Speak later,' Harrison replied. He fully intended to call her and speak to her, but when he got off the phone, there was an email in his inbox from Ryan and all thoughts of calling Tanya went out of his mind.

The second he saw the email from Ryan, Harrison knew that it was going to contain some potential leads. His assistant only ever used emojis when he was genuinely excited, and this email had two in the subject line.

Quite apart from the fact that he and Ryan had a good understanding of how the other liked to work, Ryan also had an innate ability to find the unusual amidst a massive pile of the very ordinary. It was a trait that Harrison had drummed into him from the moment they'd started working together. Most people look, but they don't see. It was Harrison's mantra, and Ryan took pride in ensuring he saw as much as possible. Where Harrison saw signs and clues in the physical world using his tracking skills and psychology training, Ryan did the same, but in the digital world.

The first piece of information related to reports of graffiti. These were very minor – not even reported to the police – but they'd come up on social media and in chat groups.

'Spot the Durham student's graffiti', was one post, with a photograph of a wall daubed with the words, '*Ne fais pas ce que tu voudras*'. Ryan had kindly translated it for Harrison: *Do not do what you want*. He hadn't needed to though; Harrison had seen a similar quote many times before.

There were other examples of the same message, and they had all been daubed on walls around the area that most of the monk sightings had occurred. Harrison knew they were connected.

The last piece of information sent through by Ryan made for even more ominous reading. 'First-year student goes missing', was the headline in *The Northern Echo*. Eighteen-year-old Christopher Downey, son of Sir Thomas and Mary Downey, disappeared a few weeks after starting at University College, Durham. Friends said it was out of character and he hadn't told them where he was going. Ryan had added a note to Harrison confirming Christopher still hadn't turned up despite a reward being offered and an extensive search.

Almost exactly a year later, George was murdered. Perhaps he hadn't been the first victim after all.

Harrison's mind went back to his conversations with the two students earlier, and a flicker of something he'd noticed prompted him to email Ryan straight back: *Can you find any photographs of Palace Green from the time that Christopher Downey went missing?*

It was incredible how many photographs got posted on social media. Even if they'd been deleted, there were ways of finding things that most people just didn't know about. Within ten minutes Ryan came up trumps and he had what he needed. A selection of selfies and scenic images of Palace Green from a year ago – and they showed him just what he'd been looking for.

It was a long shot, but Harrison had his shoes back on and was on his way back to Palace Green within minutes.

When he got there, it was quiet. Just the odd student or group traversing the area on route to their beds. Bats swooped around the open green catching insects, and the cathedral towered up into the dark night, its magnificent facade highlighted by floodlights in the darkness.

Harrison went straight over to the rose bed. At first he'd been worried he might not be able to see in the dark, but it worked in his favour. Shadows might sometimes hide a clue, but other times, they accentuated them too. There had been something he'd seen earlier, which, combined with the new information, added up to a potentially major find.

Harrison had worked on a case a couple of years back when they had a suspect with motive and evidence that he'd killed, but no victim's body. Cadaver dogs had searched the man's property and found nothing, and the investigation had stalled. The trial was due to start, and the prosecution was looking at having to cut a deal because of the lack of a body. Meanwhile, the victim's husband was devastated and unable to work through his grief until he'd been reunited with his wife and allowed to put her to rest.

Harrison had a hunch about where the murderer might have put her, but the inquiry was out of budget and time and it was both too tenuous for the SIO to tie up a dog team and the weather conditions meant the dogs would have struggled to be effective, anyway. Harrison knew that there had been studies which said trained forensic archaeologists were highly accurate in detecting buried bodies, and, with his tracking skills, he had decided to read up on the subject and try himself. He had read *The Detection of Human Remains*, by Edward W. Killam, and he spoke to some experts at the University. Then he took a week off work to systematically walk the woods where he believed Susanna Richards had been buried. It took him three days in the rain and wind – and with a pounding headache from the conditions, constant concentration, and overpowering smell of pine sap – but he'd found her.

In Palace Green it would be both easier and tougher. He had one small area to consider: the rose garden. But if a body had been buried and rose bushes planted on top, then chances are it was quite deep down. There also wouldn't be any disturbed existing vegetation, like he'd seen in the woods for Susanna's grave. The soil would be uniform in colour and texture, as the whole area had been dug up at the same time. However, there would be a third clear sign that remains might be buried: a depression in the earth. As a body decomposed, the soil would collapse down and cause an indentation on the surface. After one year, he should be able to see that – and he'd noticed something when he looked earlier. It wasn't going to be foolproof, but it would be another tick on his suspicion list.

Harrison paused and closed his eyes to focus his concentration. He wanted to look with as much objectivity as possible; to not allow his mind to see random patterns and form them into what he expected to see there.

The rose bush area was about twelve feet long, and once you knew what you were looking for, it was obvious even to an untrained eye that there was a clear dip in the middle which was just over five feet long. The light from the cathedral lights was weaker here, but there was still enough to cause clear shadowing in the dip. In addition, two of the rose bushes had slightly subsided into it. To a passer-by, it would have just seemed like uneven ground, but given Harrison's suspicion, it screamed buried body.

He was on the phone to DI Steadman straight away.

John Steadman answered the phone with a groggy voice.

Harrison didn't apologise for waking him. 'How easily and quickly can you get access to a cadaver dog?'

'Dr Lane! A cadaver dog?'

Harrison gave him a moment to wake up.

'I don't know. I think we could have one on site in Durham within two hours, possibly even one. What is it?'

'It's the so-called ghost monk and a young man who went missing a year ago. It's a long shot, but one year ago there was a considerable amount of work being done on one side of Palace Green and they created a large rose bed area, exactly at the same time that a student went missing. According to the sightings of the ghost monk, he returns to that spot and sometimes lays a rose there. As I said, it might be a long shot but I think it's worth getting a dog to take a look tonight, while Palace Green is quiet.'

'You talking about the Downey lad? They searched everywhere for him. It was suspected he'd fallen in the river drunk – not the first one to have done that – but he never turned up downstream. They sent divers in but didn't find him. It wasn't our inquiry; one of the other teams dealt with it.'

'I am.'

There was a pause again at the other end of the phone while John worked through the cost and ramifications of trusting Harrison's hunch, and the impact if he didn't.

'Bloody hell, if you're right... I'll get onto the dog handler now. Meet you there in half an hour. We'll keep this between you and me for now.'

HARRISON HAD MIXED feelings about the next hour or so. He didn't want to be right because that meant another young man was dead, but on the other hand, he knew it would at least bring some closure to Christopher Downey's parents. He also didn't want to sour relations with DI Steadman. However, he had never been someone who held back on something just in case it was wrong. He didn't subscribe to fear of failure. Every situation was a learning opportunity.

Within twenty minutes, Steadman pulled up in a blue BMW estate car.

'The dog is on its way. ETA about ten to fifteen minutes,' he said to Harrison as he got out. 'Show me what we're looking at.'

'Two eyewitnesses I've spoken to said they saw the person dressed as a monk – the so-called ghost monk – enter this area from Owengate and walk over to the flower bed here. Both of them said he paused, placed a rose, or stood here a while, before heading towards the cathedral, or down the side of it, towards the river. One year ago, this rose bed wasn't here. During the works last year, they dug up all along this area.'

Harrison showed the DI his mobile phone with the images that Ryan had pulled down from the internet. 'Most importantly, you can see a dip running across the middle, an indicator that something might have decomposed and allowed the ground to collapse inward.'

John Steadman looked from Harrison to the flower bed. At first, he strained to see, but then his eyes found the contours and Harrison saw the realisation pass across his face.

'Yes, I see it. Could all be coincidence. We've still no idea who this monk is and what they're playing at.'

'Indeed, but I think they may also be responsible for some graffiti that's been appearing. I think it's all linked.'

Before the DI could ask Harrison anything further, or allow his doubts to take hold, the canine unit van drew into Palace Green. Harrison watched as DI Steadman briefed the handler, who looked over at him, then at the flower bed and nodded. It was perfect conditions for the dog. If there was anything there, it should find it.

The handler unlocked the back of the van and disappeared for a few moments, before a large German shepherd jumped down, tail wagging with nose, eyes and ears ready for action. He was a gorgeous dog with a long silky black and tan coat, and he knew he was about to be put to work and was excited.

The handler had him on a thick leather lead, motioned to Harrison and John to move away from the area, and got the dog to sit. He did as commanded, his tail sweeping the floor and his eyes not leaving his handler's face.

The officer whispered something to the dog and unhooked the lead, letting the dog loose.

It was all over in less than two minutes. The dog sniffed the air, moved purposefully towards the flower bed, nose to the ground, gave it a few more sniffs and then spun round and sat on his haunches, facing his handler, tail wagging frantically. Not budging.

'Shit!' was all DI Steadman could manage.

BY THE TIME Duke the cadaver dog had been rewarded with a play and lots of praise from his handler, the first police cars had arrived, with Forensics not far behind them. As Duke went off shift for a well-earned sleep, an entire team set about turning the rose bed into a sealed crime scene, erecting a tent over it and bringing in specialist equipment. The DI was on the phone to the top brass at the university and cathedral, and his boss was also on his way down to ensure they didn't rub anyone up the wrong way.

Speed was essential. They wanted to secure the area and double-check Duke's prognosis before hundreds of nosy students woke up the next morning and started sharing the gossip on social media. There were still plenty of journalists in town too, sniffing around, hungry for their next headline. Chances were they'd be appearing shortly after dawn with their cameras and chequebooks. The police also wanted to ensure that the killer had as little pre-warning as possible.

Harrison stepped into the background. He was convinced he and Duke were right. He'd need to see if the remains held any further clues, but they were a while away from that stage. For now, there was nothing further for him to do. He had to let Forensics do their jobs and carefully excavate the area to avoid losing any evidence. He walked back to his hotel through the streets of Durham city and along the riverbank, and thought about the parents who tomorrow would get a phone call they'd been dreading.

13

H arrison had set his alarm early. He wanted to ensure he made the most of the momentum that finding Christopher Downey's remains would give the inquiry. He checked his phone the second his eyes were open. There was a text from DI John Steadman that said simply, *You and Duke were right. Excavating now and sent DNA for analysis.*

There had been a lot of information to take in and process yesterday. Now, he wanted to sit down, work out the jigsaw of clues and find the missing pieces. He could imagine that the incident room would be a hive of activity as their inquiry took a totally new turn. For one thing, they were going to have to consult with the original team who'd searched for Christopher, then try to find links between the two inquiries.

Harrison sent a text to DS David Urquhart and asked him to provide all the documents he could relating to that original inquiry. It was early, just gone 6 a.m., and the hotel breakfast wasn't even being served yet. DS Urquhart emailed over some of the reports he needed, and Harrison took the opportunity to sit in the peace of his room to read them and digest the information without interruptions.

Just over an hour later, Harrison saw the first light of the day creeping around the gaps in the curtains. He wasn't ready for breakfast yet and so instead of heading downstairs to the restaurant, he decided to take a walk along the river; clear his head, rest his eyes, and try to think.

The river reflected the pale orange of the sky, peach in the centre, with the dark shadows of trees mirrored along its edges. A slight mist hovered in places, giving an almost ethereal look. It was at times like this, when a new day dawned and life woke up around him, that Harrison thought most of the human cost he had to face in his work. Two young men, their lives ahead of them, would never wake up to the beauty of a morning like this one. Away from the traffic coming over the bridge, it was quiet, just the sound of bird calls and the gentle flow of water. Occasionally a rowing quad or eight sped by, their progress barely making a sound apart from the odd bark from a cox, or the occasional swish of a poor oar stroke.

He watched birds flying low over the water, their reflections shimmering and swaying on its surface, and he breathed in the cool air. It had that smell of being next to a river, earthy, with a hint of the aquatic life that inhabited it. The ground was damp, but he was in jogging bottoms and would change at the hotel before work, so he found a tranquil spot and sat down.

If, as suspected, the body on Palace Green turned out to be Christopher Downey, then it made sense that whoever was dressing up as a monk had a connection to him and either wanted to draw attention to his death, or was visiting it as some kind of homage to his own work. Harrison had come across killers like that before. They would go to funerals, hang around grave sites and revisit the scenes of their crime because it gave them just a little of the kick that the original kill had given them. Also, if the ghost monk was the killer, they could be flaunting the fact that Christopher was buried under everyone's noses and yet nobody knew he was there. Perhaps they even wanted him to be found so they could revel in the attention his murder would get and therefore how clever they had been in concealing it for all this time. It also meant that Harrison and the team could be looking at a serial killer.

The only fly in his theories were the other sightings of the ghost monk which weren't around Palace Green. Was there another crime site? Another unknown victim? Or was this where the monk lived? While the police had mapped the sightings, they were getting more and more random, with no pattern to the ghost monk's movements. The earliest sightings said the monk appeared in the Palace Green area and disappeared there too, which suggested that they might live in the vicinity, or that they were adept at avoiding CCTV and disguising themselves. He needed to track the other sightings; speak to the witnesses and double-check there were no other potential crime scenes. Sandra's daughter Gemma was one of these witnesses, plus he'd promised to speak to her and see how she was. Gemma was going to be on his priority 'to-do' list for today.

A text coming through on his phone from DS David Urquhart broke through his thoughts: *Briefing at 8:30 a.m. Well done on the find, D.*

Harrison headed back to his hotel, grabbed some breakfast, and was in the incident room by eight twenty-five. The entire room was on fire: phones ringing, officers rushing back and forth, background chatter. He could see DI Steadman talking to another detective in his office. Two minutes later, an older officer, who Harrison presumed was the assistant chief constable based on the badges on his uniform, walked through the incident room. Officers parted like the Red Sea as he approached the DI's office and entered. There were handshakes, an intense conversation, which included a glance from all three men in Harrison's direction, and then lots of nodding.

At eight forty-five, DI Steadman looked at his watch and left his office, leaving the other two to continue their conversation.

'Briefing now, everyone, please,' he shouted to the room.

Bodies poured like an hourglass from the larger room into the briefing room, filling the seats and leaving standing room only for the stragglers. Steadman flicked on the screen at the front of the room and images of the freshly excavated rose garden appeared.

'OK. Firstly, a big well done to Dr Lane for identifying the site of these buried remains. It is highly likely that it is missing student, Christopher Downey, who some of you may remember disappeared a year ago. We're waiting on DNA results, but from what we've seen of the remains so far, it fits. I obviously don't need to tell you that this means we could now be looking for a serial killer. We need to take another look at any other missing person reports over the last two or three years to ensure there are no other victims that have gone under the radar. The body was wrapped in a monk's habit, so we have a definite link. Initial indications, however, suggest he was totally doused in bleach to thwart forensic examination, which is different to how George was presented.'

A collective rustle and murmur went around the room at the mention of the monk's habit and bleach.

'We obviously had no reason to link his disappearance to our inquiry before, because it was thought Christopher had been drunk and accidentally fallen into the river. So, what is the connection between Christopher and George? Why were they both dressed as monks? Is this some kind of perversion the murderer has? Our so-called ghost monk, maybe? Is he dressing them as monks for his own reasons? I want every resource put into looking at Christopher's background, what was going on at the time he went missing, and who were his friends. Could he have been part of a secret society that Dr Lane mentioned yesterday? We will get every assistance we need from our colleagues who looked at the original disappearance.'

'Sir, any idea of when we'll get confirmation that it's Christopher?' one detective asked.

'I'm hoping within the next twenty-four hours. Obviously, there's not a lot left for us to use to ID him, so we are also chasing dental records. I'm not sure we're going to get a good idea of the cause of death either. I'm leaving Dr Sharma to work his magic. He'll let us know as soon as he has anything.'

Harrison thought about the pathologist and the delicious smell of his ginger chai. His morning would not be a pleasant one and he'd need his warm elixir to help him today.

'Dr Lane, do you have any thoughts yet as to what the monk connection might be? We obviously all know that Durham was founded by monks, but is there something more?'

'I have a working theory which relates to both the

symbols found on George and some other evidence,'
Harrison said, standing up and moving to the front of the
room. He'd sent the graffiti images to David earlier and asked
that they be circulated and put onto the briefing screen.

'There have been several cases of graffiti around the
Castle area of town. They haven't been reported to authorities
– they've just been dealt with by the property owners – but
we've found four instances, all around Saddler Street and
Moatside. *Ne fais pas ce que tu voudras,* which means *Do not do
what you want.* In this form, it means nothing other than the
message it is conveying, but it is the negative statement to
something which has much greater meaning and has been
used many times over the years: "Fais ce que tu voudras". "Do
what thou wilt", or "what you want". Has anyone seen this
before?'

Harrison scanned the faces in the room, hoping it might
trigger a memory from someone. Blank expressions stared
back and then one detective's face changed.

'It's a Celine Dion song, isn't it?'

That hadn't been what Harrison had been hoping for.

'I'm not sure about that, but what I do know is that this
motto has been linked to the Hellfire Clubs and also to
occultist Aleister Crowley.'

The faces got blanker, all apart from Lucy, the young
detective constable Harrison had sat next to in the last
briefing.

'The Hellfire Clubs, weren't they a bunch of rich lords
who used to get drunk and have Satanic sex orgies in caves?'
The second she'd finished saying the words, she turned the
colour of a tomato and clamped her lips shut in embarrassment. All eyes swivelled to Lucy and then back to Harrison.
She'd whet their tabloid clickbait instincts.

'You're on the right track. Originally, the quote was the title of a proverb by Rabelais, a French Renaissance writer, and monk. It was later used by the Hellfire Club as their motto, and then by Aleister Crowley's Thelemic occult movement. The Hellfire Club was an infamous high society social club. The most famous one was Sir Francis Dashwood's, which met in the mid-1700s. He also called it the Brotherhood, or the Friars of St Francis of Wycombe, and it then became the Monks of Medmenham Abbey after they started meeting there. They then cut tunnels and caves into the hills around High Wycombe and they met there. He even had a portrait of himself commissioned where he was dressed as a monk. At their meetings they allegedly had mock religious ceremonies, and drank and ate to excess, while also entertaining prostitutes. This obviously all ties in with the monk theme.'

Harrison looked at the faces around the table. They were still listening. That was a good sign.

'Then there's Aleister Crowley, who also used this motto in the late 1800s and early 1900s. Crowley was an interesting man. Educated at Cambridge, he rejected his parents' fundamental Christian ways and turned to ceremonial magic, studied other religions and eventually wrote a book, *The Book of the Law* which he said was dictated to him by a supernatural entity. This book said that followers should "Do what thou wilt", and it became the basis of his occult religion, Thelema, which is said to have inspired Wicca and modern paganism and Satanism.'

The watching detectives all nodded. It had piqued their interest.

'These are all historic examples, though. Why would it be used here today?' Steadman asked.

'The roots are historic, but both do still exist today. Dashwood's nephew started the Phoenix Society or Phoenix Common Room dining club at Oxford University in honour of his uncle and that is still going, plus there are said to be a number of Hellfire clubs in existence in Ireland today. Crowley's Thelema religion also has its followers. They're both very much alive, and I'm wondering if we have some kind of group inspired by one or both, here in Durham.'

'We certainly have dining clubs here. We get the occasional criminal damage claims made by hotels and restaurants where a bunch of students with more money than manners have trashed the place. Usually doesn't go to court because they just flash the cash and settle the damage,' Steadman said.

'I'm thinking the club might be a bit darker.'

'What, like some kind of satanic human sacrifices?' DI Steadman's eyebrows crossed in disgust at the thought.

'I don't know yet. The graffiti seems to contradict what the group stands for and the symbols carved onto George suggest justice and revenge. We could have some kind of society that is targeting students, or a student society that is being targeted. I need to know more about Christopher, and I need to speak to those who have seen the ghost of the monk after George was killed.'

HARRISON RETURNED to the incident room to double-check the addresses he needed to visit to interview further ghost witnesses. The meeting had broken up with a babble of enthusiasm and he could hear officers discussing potential new lines of inquiry. While the stakes had doubled with the discovery of Christopher, it also meant double the chance that they might find a clue which would give them the break-through they needed.

He was concentrating on his screen when he became aware of someone hovering around him. It was DC Lucy Armstrong.

Harrison stopped what he was doing and looked up at her. 'Do you need me?'

She blushed again, something which was clearly a daily hazard with her pale skin and shyness. 'I wondered, well, I was just wondering how you knew that Christopher's body would be there? I've looked at all the ghost monk reports and I couldn't see how you could have worked that out.' Lucy looked nervous, as though she was terrified Harrison might bite her head off.

He gave her one of his smiles. Her enthusiasm and inquisitive mind was an excellent sign of a young woman who had a great career ahead of her. 'A lot of it is looking at witness psychology and also I think we have entered a stage of social hysteria regarding the monk, so the first thing was to draw some clear timelines.'

She instantly relaxed, nodded eagerly and drew up a chair next to him. She looked tiny, sitting alongside Harrison. In her early twenties, Lucy was petite and her freckles made her look several years younger than her age.

'Nobody had made an official report until after the news broke about George's murder, so we had a time lag of a couple of weeks between the first sightings and them giving statements. There were a couple of the so-called early sightings which I discounted.' Harrison pulled up some documents on the screen to show her. 'The language used in these was vague and very much focused on the individual who was making the statement. While I'd expect some lapse of detail, there are some critical elements which they struggled to clarify and were the same descriptions you'd find on social media. I think these individuals either imagined they'd seen the monk, or were saying they had to get attention.'

Lucy looked at the screen and screwed up her eyes, concentrating. He gave her a moment.

'Here, can you see? There's a little too much vagueness and perhaps when you were interviewing them, you might have had to clarify points with them more than you would with other reports?'

She nodded slowly. 'Yes. I remember her. She was very quiet and nervous.'

'OK, so once we boil the pre-murder sightings down to those that appear to be more genuine, we end up with a few strong candidates. What we then have to remember is that by the time they've come in to you, everyone is talking about the "ghost monk". There will have been hundreds of comments on social media and it would have been incredibly hard to disassociate those stories from their genuine memories. In fact, the witnesses would be unaware that what they've since heard has become a part of their own memories. So, the best way to get them to go back in time is to take them to the place where they experienced the event. I spoke to two students who had mentioned the monk walking around Palace Green, but once on site, they were able to pinpoint more accurately where exactly the monk had walked. That led me to the rose garden. It gave a purpose to why the monk was there. Then it was a case of me looking carefully at that area to see if I could find a reason.'

'Wow.'

'You can't always take people back to crime scenes for

obvious reasons, but in this case, it was possible, and it helped,' Harrison said to her.

Lucy beamed back at him.

'Have you undertaken the cognitive interview technique training?' Harrison asked her.

'Yes, it was so interesting.'

'I can suggest some additional resources if you want to look into it in more detail.'

'Yes please, that would be great,' she replied eagerly, her eyes shining.

Harrison had found a new fan. He was delighted at her enthusiasm. The better trained the police were at interviewing, the more likely they were to catch the criminals and avoid miscarriages of justice from faulty eyewitness statements. Interview techniques had come on a long way since the 60s, 70s, and even 80s, and psychologists had played a big part in bringing about the change.

His next task was going to need more delicate handling, but it was something he had promised to do.

14

Gemma had texted Harrison to say that she could meet him for coffee that morning in between her lectures. He wanted her to show him where she'd seen the ghost monk and so they'd agreed to meet at the Billy B, which she informed him was the Bill Bryson library. There was a cafe inside, but Gemma said she'd meet him outside. He wondered if she wanted to avoid an embarrassing moment in front of other students, but when he arrived at the building, he realised it was probably more to do with practicalities. There was a constant stream of backpack-laden students filtering in and out.

He'd let Sandra know he was meeting her daughter, and she'd sent him over a photo so he could recognise her. Harrison suspected she would probably have done the same with a photo of him to Gemma. There weren't many images of him, but she could easily get hold of his police ID photograph. He wasn't somebody who it was easy to miss or not identify. A career as a spy would have been a no-hoper for Harrison. The best spies were those who weren't easily remembered, people who could merge into the background or not be identified in a sea of faces. Harrison was not one of those men.

The Billy B was a large, shiny glass-fronted building unlike the traditional structures of the Palace Green area he'd been expecting. It had more in common with his hotel. This was the modern face of Durham University, the cutting-edge research and academic facilities that somehow melded with its heritage. It also hid the area's traditional past, built on an old colliery site which was just one of many stretching across the county, taking coal from what was known as the Durham coalfield. Mined for centuries, it was the industrial revolution which led to its expansion, helping the Bishop of Durham and the major landowners of the area get rich while the miners often worked in appalling and dangerous conditions.

As Harrison watched the students streaming in and out of the modern library, he tried to imagine the old machinery and wooden structures which would have been there and the coal-coated miners, returning from the depths of the earth, coughing up the dust they'd taken down into their lungs and struggling to adjust their eyes to the sunlight as they came off shift. What would they have thought of this crystal-clear facade, full of books and papers?

Gemma was on time and gave him a quick wave and nervous smile in greeting. 'My mum's told me all about you,' she said, eyeing him up inquisitively. 'Sounds like you had a really cool childhood in Arizona.'

Harrison smiled back.

'Yeah, it was. My stepfather taught me a lot of great things.'

'I had to google the Shadow Wolves, but I'd love to know how to track stuff. It must have taken you ages to learn.'

'It took me a while, it's a bit like learning to ride a bike though, you practise and practise and it's incredibly frustrating, then suddenly it all just clicks and you don't ever look back.'

Gemma looked suitably impressed. 'Do you want a coffee?' she asked, looking at the busy building.

'I'm fine, but if you want one?'

Gemma shrugged. 'Not bothered. Do you want me to show you where I saw him?' She looked away and up the road, her face losing its earlier enthusiasm.

'Yes, please.'

They started walking up the long road out of the main city which led to the hill colleges.

'I'm at Van Mildert,' Gemma said to make conversation. 'Did my mum send you up here?' she suddenly asked out of the blue.

Harrison detected something in Gemma's voice when she asked the second question.

'Yes, she asked me to come and help. She's worried about you.'

'Is she?'

There was silence between them for a few moments. Harrison hadn't heard sarcasm in Gemma's voice, on the contrary.

'How were your parents when they dropped you off?' Harrison fished.

'Dad brought me. He was a bit squishy, but it was fine.'

They walked past Durham University buildings on both sides of the road, which was lined with trees. There were a lot of new buildings at first, abutting the pavement, but as they walked up the hill, the trees grew slightly more dense.

'I was walking back to college, just gone 9 p.m. from the Billy B,' Gemma said. 'It was around here that I saw him.'

They'd reached an area where the bushes were thicker, and it was difficult to see the buildings behind.

Gemma looked away from Harrison and stared at the path ahead. 'He just appeared in front of me. It was scary.'

'Can you tell me what happened?'

Gemma turned back round to Harrison, but looked away as she spoke.

'Yeah, so I got to about here and he just appeared. I didn't even hear the bushes move. I looked up and there he was in front of me. He had a black monk's cloak on, but under his hood, there was no face. It was like he was headless.' Gemma stared, glassy-eyed, up the road. 'I stopped, terrified, and he just stood there, looking at me, and then kind of lunged towards me. I screamed and ran.'

'Did he follow?'

'I don't know, I was so scared I just ran and didn't look back, but when I got to college, there was no sign of him.'

Harrison thought for a few moments and studied Gemma's face. 'You didn't report it to the local police, did you?'

'No. I called Mum once I'd calmed down.'

'Did the monk say anything or make any noises?'

She shook her head.

'What kind of height was he?'

'Definitely taller than me,' she said. 'I'm five eight. He was a good couple of inches taller.'

Harrison thought carefully about how to handle the next few questions he wanted to ask.

'Show me where you were, and where the ghost was. I'll be the ghost.'

'So, he was standing where you are, and I was walking up and got to about here.' She demonstrated walking up the path and stopping around two feet from Harrison, who was ahead of her.

'Then what happened next?'

'I was shocked, really frightened. I'd heard people were seeing him all over Durham and that a student had been murdered. I just ran up the hill to college as fast as I could.' Gemma trailed off, her voice growing quieter.

Harrison could see she'd realised the flaw in her story. He wasn't going to press the point now.

'Thank you, Gemma, I appreciate your time. It must have been very upsetting. Apart from this experience, are you enjoying being here otherwise?'

'Yes, it's great.' Her face brightened, and he could see the relief flow through her that he'd changed the subject. 'I love it here, the place, the course. I've made some brilliant new friends. It's such a great university, and it gets better every week.'

'It's certainly a special city. I won't take any more of your time.'

'It was nice to meet you.' She smiled at him, her eyes searching his face, hoping to see what he was thinking.

Harrison could see the threads of her mother woven through her and embroidered into her smile. He wondered if she knew he'd report back to Sandra. Probably – in fact, definitely.

'It was nice to meet you too,' he replied, smiling.

Gemma turned to walk up the hill towards her college.

'Thanks, Harrison,' she added, turning and raising her hand.

He nodded back.

. . .

HARRISON'S next appointment was to three lads who had seen the ghost monk in Palace Green, and given chase. They were the only witnesses who had tried to interact with the monk apart from the girl who had been scratched, and it was also going to be interesting to hear what they had to say because their meeting came the day after George Marshwood had been found dead. All three lived out of college and the city in a house in the Shincliffe area, so he needed his bike to get there. He would have liked to get them to Palace Green, but they only had a half-hour window in which to see him before rugby practice. He thought it better to speak to them sooner rather than later.

As Harrison walked back to where he'd parked, he thought through how and what he was going to say to Sandra about Gemma. He'd leave that conversation until later, when he had some quiet time. It needed sensitive handling.

THE THREE STUDENTS lived in what had almost certainly once been an old miner's cottage. It wasn't ample in size, but it was solid enough to withstand the three strapping, rugby-playing lads who welcomed him in. Inside, it was classic student accommodation. Not overly well kept, old furniture which was tough rather than aesthetic, and an array of eclectic items which had been taken to fancy-dress parties, acquired from various locations, or bought for their novelty value. It was all harmless fun.

Harrison scanned the room they showed him into. The lads had obviously made a cursory attempt to tidy up. He could see wipe marks where they'd attempted to eradicate the dust and beer spills, but not so successfully as to hide the fact that certain items had been removed from view. Possibly they'd been deemed inappropriate for a guest to see. The relaxed atmosphere and aroma of men's sweat and body spray mixed in with stale pizza and beer, reminded Harrison of being a student; it seemed all too long ago now.

The three students –Toby, Richard, and Matthew – looked like they were enjoying the attention their heroic efforts at catching the ghost had brought them. They were eager to tell him their story. All three were above average in height and build, and Richard's ears carried the signs of scrum scarring, despite the protection they wore these days.

'Not a huge amount of space,' Matthew said, looking around the sitting room for somewhere for their guest to sit. It wasn't often they were outsized. Harrison sat down opposite them.

'Nice cottage,' he said to break the ice. Small talk wasn't his forte, but he recognised it was needed sometimes.

'Yeah. Solid walls which help with the neighbours. Last place we had was a new build with paper-thin walls, our neighbours were constantly complaining about noise. We couldn't even sit and have dinner together without them moaning we were waking their kids up.'

Harrison wondered what kind of level of dinner noise they considered reasonable and at what hour, but decided not to pursue that one.

'Can you tell me what you saw?'

'It was the day after George Marshwood got murdered. We'd already heard stories about some strange ghost that was haunting Palace Green, and it had attacked a girl,' said Matthew.

'Yeah, and everyone was jumpy cos they knew that George was found dressed as a monk,' chipped in Toby.

'We were coming back from the Undie – we'd been for drinks with some mates from rugby – and we saw him.'

All three nodded earnestly at Harrison.

'We just kind of decided to see if we could arrest him. Didn't believe he was a ghost. Looked solid enough to us.'

Harrison's turn to nod.

'So, we shouted, and he started to run.'

'Yeah, shouting probably wasn't the smartest move,' said Richard. 'Stealth isn't our strong point.' He smirked.

'Toby here's a winger. Can turn on the speed when you need to, can't you, mate,' Matthew said. 'He got ahead of us two, but the monk was pretty fast too.'

'Yeah, and light. We lost him. One minute he was there and the next he wasn't. The only way he could have got away was by vaulting a wall and that wouldn't have been easy.'

'He just disappeared? Where exactly?'

'He was along the far side away from the castle, and I think he looked like he was going to run towards the cathedral, but we were too quick and cut him off, so instead he darted into Bailey Court,' said Toby.

'Could he have gone into one of the buildings?' Harrison asked.

They all shook their heads.

'We tried every door. There was nowhere for him to go. He wouldn't have had time to unlock a door or anything like that.'

'Did any of you get a look at the person, or can you describe their build?'

They all looked at one another.

'Shorter than us and thinner,' Matthew said to the other two's nods. 'Couldn't see a face at all.'

'You've said "him" all the way through. What makes you say that?'

All three wrinkled their chins and thought.

'If I'm honest,' said Richard, looking at the other two, 'I think it was more like the build of a woman.'

'Yeah, I'd agree,' Toby said, nodding.

Harrison knew that interviewing witnesses in a group was far from ideal. Co-witness information was extremely influential and could change an individual's memory of an event. The three lads could have totally false memories of that night, brought about by reinforcing each others' versions. Add to this the fact that witnesses tend to be inaccurate when judging the height and weight of people, and more often than not use their own height and weight as the marker to judge other people by. With these three all above average in body build, that could mean the ghost was an average or above average individual too.

'This wasn't in your original statement,' Harrison said to them.

They exchanged glances again.

'No. I think we were a bit pumped with the chase. I don't think I really thought about it, but it was the way they ran and their size,' Toby added.

'Tobe was up front. He got the best look,' Matthew said.

'Thank you for your honesty,' Harrison said. There was no reason for Toby to suggest the ghost had been female. If anything, it would detract from their macho chasing down of a murderer. Why ruin a good story unless you really believed it? Harrison added the information to his list of clues.

'Anything else you may have thought about afterwards?'

The three of them pursed their lips and furrowed their brows.

'There was one thing which we remembered, but not sure it's relevant,' Matthew said.

'Anything could be relevant,' Harrison replied.

'Yeah, but it's not related to the monk,' Matthew continued, 'it's about George.'

Harrison nodded to encourage him.

'He played rugby with us in the first term. Was OK, nothing special, and he dropped out after Christmas. We never saw him again. We're all Hatfield, so paths just didn't cross. But...' Matthew hesitated again. 'Well, it's odd, but there was one week when he couldn't play. His legs and back were so bruised. It was bizarre.'

'Yeah, we all saw it. I think the coach spoke to him about it. You know, wondered if he'd been self-harming or if someone had attacked him. He said he'd fallen down the stairs and it never got mentioned again. Just seemed odd like, you know?'

'Were you aware of George being in any secret societies?'

The three lads looked at each other. The atmosphere became a little more tense.

'We didn't know him that well.'

'Do you know of any societies he could have been in?'

'There's a few, you know, mostly dining groups. The Castle Fives maybe, but like we said, we didn't know him that well.'

The lads shifted uncomfortably, and Harrison guessed he was getting too close to the bone. He didn't want to lose their cooperation, so he dropped the subject.

'What was the name of the rugby coach who spoke to George?'

'Err, that would have been Bob Enson, he's still with the university team. We're all in the Durham firsts now but at the time we were Freshers and in the devs squad.'

Harrison looked quizzical.

'Developmental squad, it's where you start out while they assess you.'

Harrison made a note to follow this up. It might be nothing, but he had a suspicion, and that told him it was definitely worth looking into.

15

I t turned out Bob Enson was at work and not
contactable until later on, so Harrison left a message
and asked him to call. For the rest of the afternoon, he
read through the original case files for Christopher Downey.
The team were working hard, searching for potential connec-
tions. Apart from the fact they both went to the same college
and had similar backgrounds – wealthy families and private
school educations – their paths didn't seem to cross. Seeing
as around a third of Durham students went to private
schools, that wasn't a big enough link.

College authorities had been contacted and there were no
records for any societies or associations, informal or formal,
dining or otherwise, which related to monks. There were
several so-called secret societies mentioned and the team
were checking these out, but none of them appeared to have
the initials of two Ms, that linked to George. If this society did
exist, it had to be relatively new.

Once Harrison returned to his hotel room, he kicked off
his shoes and stripped down to his boxers. Then he took a

few of the cushions from the bed and put them on the floor, where he sat on them cross-legged. For fifteen minutes he slowed his breathing, from deep lung-filled rhythmic ins and outs, to a barely noticeable raise of his well-defined chest.

The aim wasn't to calm his breathing but to still his mind – bring it back from the frenzy of data and information inputs he'd been soaking up that day. Twenty-four hours ago they were looking for the killer of a twenty-year-old student, now they had two bodies and a potential serial killer on their hands.

The so-called ghost was clearly anything but. The big question was, were they the killer? There had been a couple more sightings of the ghost monk last night, but Harrison was seeing a clear division in the reports and victims. There were those who had seen the monk on Palace Green. Their stories were all very similar and while he couldn't discount that some of them may have read other peoples' accounts, or know another witness, he had a group that seemed to be fairly trustworthy in terms of witness reliability. Then there were the others, and amongst the 'others' was Gemma Barker.

Harrison picked up his mobile and dialled Sandra's number. It took a few rings before she picked up the call, and he heard the sounds of someone playing a saxophone in the background.

'Harrison!' Sandra said, 'How's it going in Durham?'

The sound of the music grew fainter. Sandra was obviously at home. He knew her husband and son, Raff, were both very musical. He could imagine her walking into another room so she could hear him and concentrate on the call.

'We have another body. Just been confirmed as that of a student who went missing a year ago.'

'Oh crap. Are you making any headway?'

'Slowly.'

'You've been to see Gemma, she tells me. She called you an "imposing figure", a term which my daughter isn't known to use often. In fact, I've never heard her say it before. So, how was she?'

'She is absolutely fine. You have nothing to worry about. She seems to be really enjoying it here.'

'I feel a *but* coming.'

'I think it would be nice for you and her if you came up and let her show you around.'

There was silence on the other end for a while as Sandra tried to extract the meaning from between the lines of what Harrison had just said.

'Are you being honest with me? Is she really OK? Has something else happened?'

'I promise you that as far as I can tell, she's absolutely fine. She really likes it and I think would enjoy sharing her enthusiasm with you and having your company and full attention.'

'And the ghost attack?'

'I seriously wouldn't worry about that. That's under control.'

More silence.

'OK, I see. I should be able to get away next weekend. I'd really hoped to be able to take her up there with Sam, but it just didn't happen. She's been asking for a couple of jumpers that she'd left behind. I was going to post them, but I'll take them myself instead. Raff has a lot of rehearsals for a concert over the next few weekends. Sam can stay here with him, and

I'll go spend a couple of days with Gemma. Just the two of us.'

'I think she'd appreciate that.'

'OK, thank you Harrison. I hope I haven't dragged you into a nightmare case up there.'

'Not at all. It's a nice city and, you know me, I love a good mystery.'

Harrison was relieved he'd made the phone call. Sandra had taken it well and reacted exactly as he'd hoped. He shouldn't have expected anything different. He was also glad she didn't quiz him further about Gemma's 'ghost experience'. His message had been subtle, but he'd managed to get across all that was needed to be said.

With that weight off his shoulders, Harrison put on his running gear and left the hotel for a run by the river. It was a different experience to his usual riverside one in London. Quieter, fresher and alongside a river that felt more intimate and approachable in size. His energy levels were different here, too. He noticed the lack of tension in his run. He pushed himself, but it was because he wanted to rather than that he needed to. The pace of life was slower here, and it transferred to him. His mind wandered to Leo Fawcett, and then to Tanya. He'd call her as soon as he'd got back and showered.

Harrison caught sight of the cathedral tower and admonished himself for not focusing on the job. He was here to find a killer and so far all he'd done was find another victim. He passed under Elvet Bridge and slowed to a walk. This was the area where the police believed George had been murdered and put into the boat. They'd searched, but found nothing.

Harrison knew it would be too late to glean much, if anything at all, from any signs he could see now. Police officers and dogs had been trampling the undergrowth and anyone could have been here contaminating the scene. He looked anyway, just in case.

He could see where feet had trampled the undergrowth, and there was evidence that a larger object had crushed plants. Could this be where George was incapacitated? He dropped to a crouch and looked closely at the earth. There were some faint lines drawn into the ground. There were four of them parallel to each other, and they were about six inches or so in length.

His mind jumped back to what Sunil had said. *There was some debris under his nails which looked like they had been scraped across a hard surface and mud, but I am thinking that was probably inflicted when he was dying in agony from the poison.* Could this be where George had scratched at the earth in agony?

Harrison looked around him. Trees sheltered the river-bank. If the killer had wanted to just kill George, he could have pushed him into the water to drown once the poison was taking effect, but they didn't. They'd gone for the dramatic option of floating him down the river in a boat. His death was a statement. A message that whatever he had done would not be tolerated.

How did the ghost monk fit into all this? Harrison had asked Toby to pinpoint on the map the exact location he or she had disappeared when they were being chased. He'd go and take a look now, but rather than retrace his steps, he'd follow the tiny lane that led from the riverbank to Saddler Street. Could that be the route that George and his killer had taken?

Harrison walked into Palace Green. The crime scene that was once the rose garden sat like an open sore. Forensics had finished, but the area was still cordoned off by police tape. A handful of students stood looking and talking. There was no doubting the main topics of conversation in the student bars and online chat boards. Ryan was monitoring them like a hawk. All they needed was some kind of clue as to what sort of society they were dealing with. His fear was that the 'message' George's killer had sent had forced those who did know something to clam up.

He arrived at the spot in Bailey Court where the ghost was alleged to have disappeared. He could see what the lads meant. Buildings rose up around him, apart from a large wall in front. To scale that you would have to be very nimble. He'd be able to do it at a push just because he had good upper body strength, but the average person, especially a female, would find it near impossible to pull up their own weight. No wonder witnesses said the so-called ghost seemed to vanish into thin air. He looked around at the windows overlooking the area. All had locks, which would prevent them from being opened and allowing somebody inside. That's not to say that the monk hadn't pre-prepped a window, but it was highly unlikely. They had been cut off from their usual escape route, and so this wasn't where they'd have expected to end up. Harrison would try to find out if there was any CCTV for this area and beyond the wall. See if anyone was picked up on it that night.

He'd come up with a brief profile of George's killer for the police, but he was far from satisfied with it. There was very little to go on. The killer clearly had a sadistic streak; the method of death, cutting the symbols into his chest, and quite possibly the tattoo was their handiwork. They were also confident and enjoyed being the centre of attraction, and, most importantly, they were a control freak. Putting George into a boat and staging him took courage, or a misplaced messiah mentality. Yet Harrison was pretty sure it was another student. George would have been unlikely to have been drinking with someone who wasn't in his age group and social circle.

His priority had to be meeting the lads who'd lived with George. Could one of them be his killer?

Harrison's mobile buzzed on his arm where he'd strapped it for his run. When he pulled it free, he saw Tanya's name.

'Tanya, I was going to call you when I got back to the hotel.'

'Is now not convenient?'

'No, it's fine. I'm walking back now so we can talk.'

'How's it going? I've seen the story in the papers about some phantom monk who is terrorising the city.'

'Mm, I think it's a bit more complicated than that, but there is certainly a fair bit of histrionics going on here right now.'

'I bet you're loving that.'

For a moment he thought Tanya was being serious, and then he heard the humour in her voice.

'So, any ideas how much longer you'll be?'

'Not yet. We've got another victim, but don't seem to be any closer to finding the killer.'

'I've got to go to a black tie awards evening, night after tomorrow. I'd hoped you might be able to join me, but it's fine if you can't make it. The guy who is organising the table said he'd find someone to take my second ticket if you were still away.'

Harrison thought about the image of her in an evening dress, and then of spending an evening at an awards ceremony. While being in Tanya's company would definitely be an enjoyable experience, he was absolutely sure that getting dressed up, and sitting with a table full of strangers and having to make polite small talk while they all probably slipped into varying stages of alcoholic revery, would not. Besides, he didn't even own a dinner suit; he'd have to hire one.

'I think that's probably the best idea,' he said.

'OK. No problem.'

He heard the disappointment in her voice and was glad that he had a solid work excuse and hadn't just told her he didn't want to go because it wasn't his thing.

He was walking up Saddler street, and had reached the Flat White cafe where he'd stood with DS Urquhart on his first night here. It reminded him that they'd not been able to hear each other because workmen were power washing the wall. While Tanya talked about some new equipment that had arrived that day in the laboratory, he focused his attention around him.

He couldn't see any graffiti left on that wall. The guys had done a good clean-up, but as he walked past the opening to a narrow lane that was more like an alleyway than anything, he saw three letters on the wall. *FFF*. They looked simple and innocuous, but Harrison knew they could mean something that was quite otherwise. He walked down the passageway, searching on the floor and walls for any other symbols. There was random graffiti – a few different names sprayed on the walls with varying degrees of artistic talent, and the odd impolite message to the government. Then, about fifty yards along, outside a door, an area caught his interest. Someone had clearly tried to scrub off two pieces of graffiti, but they hadn't done as thorough a job as the power hose because flecks of paint had clung to the brick wall. If you'd walked past, you wouldn't have noticed them, but Harrison wasn't a normal passer-by. First, he was focusing on the wall, and second, he was trained in tracking and reading signs that the average individual would never even see.

The wall appeared to carry a random series of white paint flecks. To Harrison, he could clearly see that one was the upside-down pentagram, and the other was the symbol that George had tattooed onto his body: of what appeared to be a capital *M* and lower case *m* in the Greek alphabet.

'Harrison? Harrison? Are you still there?' Tanya returned to his ear as the impact of what he'd found came to him: 'F' was the sixth letter in the alphabet, sometimes used as a more subtle way of showing the devil's sign of 666, and the pentagram was unmistakeably Satanic.

The narrow passage led to the cathedral and, critically, to Palace Green. Harrison walked back quickly to where he'd entered the passageway. There on the wall was its name: Moatside Lane. Thoughts of the Medmenham Monks came to him. The Moatside Monks. That was it. It had to be the name of the group.

16

Harrison almost missed the phone call from DS Jack Salter as he got out of the shower, and in hindsight, he wished he had.

He'd needed to spend ten minutes apologising to Tanya on the way back, but the conversation hadn't gone too well. He'd not only let her down with the awards event, but he hadn't listened to a word she'd said because he'd been concentrating on looking for further symbols and signs that Moatside Lane was linked to their killer. Tanya had asked for his advice, and he'd been unable to contribute anything because he'd simply not heard what she'd said. He felt guilty for having to ask her to repeat it all again, but finding the symbols had been important.

Perhaps he could do better with Jack.

'Harrison, your witch doctor powers have worked.'

Harrison waited for the punchline of another DS Jack Salter joke, but it didn't come. This one wasn't funny.

'I've found Freda Manning, and she's in a hospice just outside of Harrogate. It's about four hours from London.'

'Hospice? Are you sure it's her?'

Harrison's heart felt like it had stopped beating.

'Yes. I've already been onto the home, and they have ID'd her from a photograph we have from an old passport. It's definitely Freda. She hasn't even tried to hide her identity.'

'Which hospice?'

'Harrison, we should go together. You need someone with you. This has to be done properly. For your sake, not hers.'

'I'm not in London. I'm in Durham. Harrogate is about an hour from here.'

'Are you working on a case? Sorry, I should have checked. I didn't mean to distract you. She's not going anywhere. I'll book us an appointment. Let's meet up there once you've wrapped up what you're doing in Durham. I'll come up and meet you.'

'Sure,' Harrison replied.

But he knew Jack had interviewed enough people in his career to know a lie when he heard one.

RYAN HAD the address for Harrison within twenty minutes. Jack had been right; she'd not tried to hide who she was. Was this another one of their traps?

Why would they be luring him to Harrogate? If Freda was there, would he find Desmond, too?

Harrison sat in the red armchair in his hotel room and stared out into the early evening dusk. All thoughts of the Durham case and Tanya had disappeared from his mind. He was barely aware of his surroundings. Something told him to be wary. It could not be this simple. He wasn't going to ride to Harrogate and find Freda repentant on her deathbed, ready to give him all the answers he'd been searching for; but he had to try. She couldn't be faking dying, although even heading towards death he could bet the pair of them would still be hatching their evil plans.

He felt sick in the pit of his stomach. A ball of fury, which had been kept under control for so long, was starting to spin again. It might be their plan to get him to go – they didn't think he'd be able to resist, and they were right. He would be up early tomorrow and ride straight down so he could be there at the PennyGate Hospice for the start of visiting hours.

HARRISON SLEPT VERY LITTLE. He kept waking every hour in case he'd missed his alarm and it was morning. In his head he'd gone over and over what he was going to say, and in his dreams Freda Manning took turns to be a cowed repentant or satanic witch. He knew which was the most likely, and that was why the nightmares kept him from rest. The Mannings' faces had swirled around his dreams. Sometimes he was chasing them, other times he was running for his life but not getting anywhere. The faster he ran, the more his body lifted up from the ground. He was rooted to the same spot he'd been in ever since his mother's death, while Freda and Desmond disappeared in the distance. Free.

As soon as it was time, he got on his bike and headed out of Durham onto the A1. He didn't give a second glance to the cathedral and castle as he left them behind. Harrison sped along the motorway, eyes firmly focused forwards, the green of the grass verge blurring along with the grey central reservation barriers. Cars occasionally went by him, but mostly he sped past them. Seeing nothing but what was in front of him.

He didn't once look either side to the rolling landscape of fields and woodlands. Greens and yellows turning to greys in the far distance, where the sky hung low to the ground. He didn't see the herds of tail swinging cows, brown and cream, or the white specks of sheep grazing across the fields. Harrison knew his destination, and there was no stopping him. He didn't hesitate until he reached PennyGate Hospice.

As he pulled into the car park, the sign for the hospice made him sneer. 'Enabling living through kindness and respect'. While he fully respected the aims of the hospice, he doubted Freda Manning had been kind to anyone in her life. She certainly didn't deserve respect. He hated the bitterness inside of him, the anger that chewed away at his insides every time he thought about the Mannings. For as long as he felt this way about them, he knew they would have control over him. He wanted to purge her from his insides. She was a cancer. A rotten, festering tumour that he needed to remove.

The brown-brick building was innocuous, hiding the daily misery of loved ones having to say their goodbyes to those who could no longer manage the pain and fight of living. There was no pain or sadness in Harrison's heart. It was cold and hard. His hands tightly fisted.

As he got off his bike, he felt the stiffness from the tension that held his body rigid. At any other time he would have stopped and tried to release that tension, brought his breathing under control and eased the fast shallow breaths which were inefficiently trying to oxygenate his body and did nothing to calm him. Today, though, he didn't want to stop for anything.

Harrison strode across the car park towards the entrance with only one thought on his mind. To find Freda Manning.

'Harrison. Harrison!' A man had run towards him and touched his elbow.

Harrison swung round in surprise. The man almost

ducked in an automatic reaction. Harrison's eyes were dark and his face set hard and tight.

'Jack!'

'I didn't want you going in there alone. It's my fault you're here, and I knew you wouldn't wait,' he said by way of explanation.

There was a moment's pause between them as the shock of the sight of each other subsided.

'Thanks to you, I had to miss my breakfast this morning and lose three hours' precious sleep.' Jack reverted to his default humorous way of dealing with anything stressful.

Harrison wasn't sure whether he felt angry at Jack for being there, or relieved. For a while, he couldn't say anything, just stared at his friend.

'Look, why don't we go and get a coffee and a mint tea first, before you go in there. We've both had long journeys, and you need to be in the right frame of mind before you see her. The last thing you're going to want is to go in there all stressed. She'll think she's got to you. You don't want that to be her last thought, do you?'

Harrison wasn't sure what he wanted right now.

Walking away from Freda Manning, when he knew she lay helpless in a bed just a hundred metres away, was a hard choice, but Harrison allowed himself to be led by Jack. He followed him silently to his car and got in, fastening his seat belt like he was some kind of android automaton.

Harrison had played the scene out in his head a thousand times on the way down. Sometimes she told him all he wanted to know, eager to leave this world with some kind of forgiveness. Other times she'd tricked him, and Desmond was waiting for him like Little Red Riding Hood's wolf. Then there were the times Harrison turned her morphine right up or right down, playing out his revenge. None of the scenarios had included Jack.

'Why are you here?' Harrison finally said to him.

Jack had his eyes on the road, but quickly glanced over at him. 'I think you know the answer.'

Harrison hadn't always managed to control his temper when faced with injustice, and for him personally, there was no greater injustice than his mother's death being labelled as suicide and her killers being allowed to wander free. Of course, he knew why Jack was here. His mind was spinning. Jack would get in the way of what he might have been capable of doing. He knew Jack would play it by the book; that was his way. Methodical and thorough. Harrison was more bull in a china shop, and Jack was there to ensure he didn't create mayhem and the potential consequences. Harrison couldn't yet bring himself to thank him for being here.

As he sat in the cafe with Jack, the dark, spinning mist in his head started to subside. He hadn't even taken any notice of where they'd ended up, he'd just followed and done as Jack had suggested. While Harrison had sat silently at a table, surrounded by couples and groups of people chatting and gossiping, Jack had ordered him a mint tea, and got himself coffee and an all-day breakfast.

'There are a few things we need to get out of today,' Jack had begun, just half a potato waffle and some streaks of egg and ketchup left on his plate. He bypassed the emotional and focused on the practical. 'First, we need to ask her about the Nunhead murder – we can mention the victim's name now. Then we can try to find out where Desmond is, and finally we obviously have to ask about your mother. If we say that we've got a witness who is prepared to testify that it wasn't suicide, then she might want to protect Desmond. I've no idea how long she has left, but a prison sentence is certainly not going to be a deterrent for her. Let's hope she's not too high on morphine and actually knows what we're talking about.' Jack finished off the waffle and looked across the table at him. 'You OK?'

Harrison was aware that he'd still barely said a word since Jack had arrived. While he was never the chattiest kind of person, even for him this silence was unusual.

'There has to be a motive behind this. Why suddenly come out into the open now?'

'Maybe she had to in order to seek medical help. If she's in pain, it can make you do desperate things.'

'Or, more likely, they're plotting something.'

'You think this is a trap?'

'I know there's something. It's in my head too, I just can't see what it is.' Harrison looked at Jack to see if he understood.

His friend was looking serious for once, and nodded slowly. 'I don't see how she can hurt you. Even if Desmond is here, they're going to have to get through me as well.'

'I'm not sure it's that straightforward.'

Harrison had to admit that taking the time out allowed him to calm down a little and be in a stronger frame of mind. His friend was right. The last thing he wanted to do was walk in there and for Freda to think she was in control.

By the time they returned to the hospice he was ready, and knowing Jack had his back gave him extra strength.

The woman at reception was full of sympathy and kind smiles. She was just the kind of person you needed to see when you first arrived at a hospice – unless you were going to see your mother's murderer. Harrison found it hard to swallow the kindness which was offered to them. He wasn't here to visit a loved one. He was here for a day of reckoning with a person who personified evil and had done her best to ruin his life. While they sat and waited, he closed his eyes to the posters which offered counselling and a shoulder to cry on, and instead took himself back to Arizona, their safe place, when he and his mother had escaped the Mannings. He focused his mind on the positive feelings those memories gave him, and he channelled his energy into keeping himself calm. It was hard, but Jack was right. He didn't want her to think she'd won by dragging him here in a state of stress.

He wasn't massively successful at the relaxation. When the door to reception opened and a nurse came in to show them the way to Mrs Manning's room, his stomach lurched so hard he thought he might be sick. As he got up to follow her, in his mind he was a little boy again, his mother walking by his side, holding his hand.

The hospice had done its best to paint the walls with bright, cheerful colours. Children's pictures of rainbows and sunshine were strategically placed next to uplifting extracts from poems and psalms. They couldn't help smother the smell of disinfectant and medical wipes, or the hush that was broken only by the sound of a bedside call bell buzzing some-where down the corridor.

'Mrs Manning is doing well,' the nurse said to Harrison and Jack. 'She has had no visitors, so I'm sure she'll be pleased to see you. She's in a shared ward with three other ladies. Once she gets closer to her time, we'll move her into an individual room.'

Neither man replied, but Harrison guessed the nurse was used to that. Family and friends would often be overwhelmed when they made their first visit.

'Here you go. Mrs Manning is in the second bed on the

left by the window. I'll check on you in about half an hour, make sure she's not getting too tired.'

Harrison looked at Alice for the first time; a badge proclaimed her given name and carried the hospice logo of two hands, one helping the other. She had long dark-blonde hair pulled back in a ponytail and was probably in her late twenties. What Harrison had failed to see initially was the convex nature of her belly, which, from its shape and positioning, showed that new life was soon to be celebrated, amid the passing of others. He briefly wondered how she managed to keep a lid on her emotions, heightened by hormones, amid such sadness. Then he was back in the stress of the here and now. He realised Jack was waiting for him to walk forwards. So he took one step after another, towards the woman he'd last seen in Nunhead Cemetery just a couple of months ago.

Freda Manning's screen was pulled around her bed so that you couldn't see her until right up close. For someone who had created so much misery in his life, she looked small and insignificant, lying vulnerable and alone, attached to an intravenous tube which snaked its way down from a bag of clear fluid and into the large blue blood vessel on the back of her bony hand. Jack hung back behind the screen and Harrison stepped forward, coming to a halt at the end of the bed. Slowly, Freda Manning opened her eyes.

'You've come,' she said to him. Her voice was thin, throat dry, and her breathing short and shallow. 'Here for some answers, are you? Or perhaps to say goodbye?' she continued, a sparkle coming back into her eyes.

'Where's Desmond?' Harrison asked.

Freda gave a half smile. 'Pass me the water, will you?'

Harrison hesitated. She stared straight back at him. He could see the sickness in her. She'd deteriorated since he'd seen her at Nunhead. Her skin had become like rice paper, and the darkness under her eyes showed the shadow of death creeping up on her. She'd lost weight too, her grey hair thinning and lank, just hung from her skull. He despised her. He walked around the side of the bed to where a beaker of water with a straw was sitting and thrust it towards her.

She took it slowly and put the straw to her dry lips to drink, not taking her eyes off his face. He knew she was goading him.

'Where's Desmond?' Harrison asked again.

Her mean mouth turned up at the corners. 'We've said our goodbyes. He won't be coming back here.' She took another sip of water. 'I bet you'd like to finish me off, wouldn't you? Be my guest.'

For a few moments the pair of them stared at each other, a standoff. Jack's shuffling pulled Freda's stare away from Harrison.

'I see you've brought back-up.' Freda gave a cursory glance towards Jack, who had moved to the bottom of the bed. 'Come to arrest me, has he?'

'We have an eyewitness who will testify that Isabel Lane could not have committed suicide in 2004. An investigation into her death is going to be reopened.' Jack didn't know this for sure, but he said it with conviction.

Freda looked away from him and back to Harrison, studying his face.

'Mrs Manning,' Jack continued, 'we would like to interview your husband in connection with the death of Isabel Lane, and also with the murder of Annette Ward at Nunhead in 1993. If you refuse to tell us his whereabouts, then you can be charged with conspiracy to pervert the course of justice.' Even as he said it, Harrison could hear the doubt in Jack's voice. He knew that threat would be ineffective in these circumstances.

Freda Manning ignored him and instead gave a twisted smile to Harrison. 'So you still don't remember, do you?'

His stomach lurched at her words. This was his biggest fear, that deep inside he had memories which he'd buried. Memories which he didn't want to revisit or acknowledge. He tried hard not to let anything show on his face.

'Go back to Nunhead. Look for a stone.'

Harrison knew exactly the place she meant and exactly what stone she was referring to. When he'd last gone back, he'd seen flashes of that night in 1993. Did he bury it because he'd liked Annette, and witnessing her death had been so traumatic for him as a child? Or was there some other reason Freda wanted him to remember?

Freda Manning started to cough. A rattling, wheezing cough of a person whose lungs were rotting. He knew her soul had rotted a long time before the cancer took hold. He watched impassively as her frail body heaved with each breath.

Freda waved Jack towards her. 'Leave your card,' she was just able to say in between coughs and gulping to get in enough air.

Jack looked at Harrison and walked to the bedside table, where he took a business card from his jacket pocket and placed it on the side.

Harrison didn't move. He stared at Freda Manning, watching the woman he hated struggle to breathe. He knew Jack was getting a little anxious, and as Freda's gasping for air became worse, he disappeared out of the room.

Freda clawed at the call button which sat by her side on the bed, her bony fingers trying to feel for the button as her mind became oxygen-starved and her body failed her. He did nothing to help her. Just stood watching. Occasionally she stopped struggling long enough to glance quickly at him. A broken human who seemed incapable of doing any harm to anyone but herself.

As the nurses rushed in to help Freda, alerted by Jack, Harrison stepped away from her bedside and walked from the room. She looked harmless, but he knew she still hadn't played her final hand. There was a defiance in her eyes that told him so. What he didn't know was what exactly her last card would deliver.

17

There were twelve missed calls on Harrison's mobile when he got back to Durham, and a huge long email from Ryan. He stared at his phone, unable to deal with any of them. He felt exhausted. Harrison wasn't somebody who slept in the day, unless he was ill, but he felt like a ton of feather mattresses had been dumped on top of him. He knew it wasn't just the disturbed sleep and journey to and from Harrogate. The biggest toll had been the emotional one. Seeing Freda, the expectation of it all and then what was essentially a pointless journey, had ripped out his insides and wrung them out like a dishcloth. He knew this feeling, and he knew it could lead to self-destruction. When he felt like this, he wanted to ditch the herbal teas and healthy living and head straight into the bar. He wanted to sit for the rest of the afternoon, drinking himself to oblivion. That way, he would be incapable of thinking about Freda Manning and what they'd done to his mother. He wouldn't have to see her evil face and those dark eyes which bored into him, searching his soul for memories which he'd buried and wanted to forget.

Andrew McKendrick's warning words came back to him. Maybe his old friend had been right: he should drop it. Should have dropped it. Harrison couldn't help but feel that something had been set in motion by his visit. Something he might regret. He texted Andrew and told him Freda was in the hospice and he'd seen her. Seconds later, he received one back.

Are you OK?

Fine, Harrison wrote.

Let's catch up again as soon as you can.

Harrison dashed off a reply that he'd call when he was back in London.

Jack had also been concerned when they'd parted company. Harrison had barely said a word to him, not because he was angry at him for being there, or for calling the nurses when Freda was coughing, but because Jack was out of place. He didn't belong in the past with the Mannings; he hadn't lived through Harrison's experiences. He was like a ghost on the film reel. Out of context. Yet it had been him who Freda had reached out to. Why had she wanted Jack's card? What was it that she had planned in her final days? Harrison appreciated that Jack had gone there to help him, but now he'd ended up being a part of it. Whatever was set to be unleashed, he hoped it wouldn't be aimed at his friend.

There was no way he could concentrate with his head the way it was, and he wasn't about to let the Mannings win by walking into the nearest pub. He had to ground himself, get his control back before he could even consider being a useful part of the Durham investigation. Right now, the Mannings had control of all his senses and that made him even more angry. He felt exhausted, but he also felt rage. The pent-up fury of someone who didn't have control over what was important to them.

Harrison had seen lots of people who felt like this in his career, particularly when he'd worked in the prisons. Sometimes it was those who had taken that rage out on another human being. Battering flesh and blood just to feel some kind of power. It was always fleeting, always unsatisfying, and they had to keep doing it over and over just to keep a lid on their anger, but never exhausting it. Then there were those who were the self-harmers, the ones who cut themselves or had eating disorders. Those who felt so out of control in their lives that the only thing they could have any control over – their body – became the object of their rage.

He wasn't about to do any of that. Harrison refused to be driven into doing anything negative or harmful, but he had to do something. He got changed and went to the hotel gym. Every muscle in his body felt tensed for flight. He was ready to go into battle, to charge at his enemy and fight for his life. He needed to run that energy out, drain his fury so that it couldn't hurt him, or anyone else.

The gym was part of a health club and so it had more equipment than many others, and there was also a good-sized pool. Nevertheless, there was only one other person in there when he arrived. A middle-aged woman who was using one of the leg-curl machines. She looked like being in the gym was helping her pass time rather than that she there for some serious exercise. She wore brand-new Sweaty Betty gym leggings and a vest, which had definitely not had the opportunity to live up to their name. She'd do five leg curls and then stop for a while and look around. When Harrison walked in, she seemed to perk up. The scenery had just got a whole lot better.

He didn't acknowledge her. He was in no mood for distractions. Instead, he walked straight to one of the running machines and got on, pressing the buttons so it beeped fast, until the speed racked up to a run. Even the irritating sound of the beeping machine gave his rage energy. He fixed his eyes forward and stared at the plain green wall in front of him, and then he ran.

He ran until every muscle in his legs and buttocks were pumped and hard, until the sweat ran down his back, darkening the black sleeveless T-shirt he wore. His shoulders shone with the exertion and his arms worked back and forth like pistons. As he ran, he punched at the air to release the tension, flexing his biceps and pushing the breath from his body with each punch. He needed more. He needed his lungs to hurt, his abs to be straining, fully extended, and so he pushed the speed higher. He wanted pain. He wanted every muscle to be screaming for him to stop.

Harrison's cheeks billowed and his face reddened as the exertion raised his body temperature. His feet pounded on the treadmill, thumping down rhythmically amid the whining whir of the machine. His entire face glistened with sweat and he could feel it starting to drip into his eyes and down the back of his thick neck, running over the small tattoo of a brown eagle.

Finally, his breathing became ragged. His lungs burnt with each inhalation and exhalation. He struggled to get the oxygen in fast enough to his tired muscles, and at last he slowed the treadmill down to a jog and then a walk. He rolled his shoulders, trying to release the last of the tightness which had held his back so rigid and caused his neck pain.

When he got off, he allowed his head to steady before stretching his legs and arms, bending from side to side and flexing his hips. Then he took it in turns to stand on one leg, bending the other up to pull his thighs and hamstrings into a stretch. Tipping onto alternate heels to work his calf muscles. For a few moments he stood still, focusing on his breathing, feeling the pumping of oxygenated blood bubbling around his system. When he'd finished, he turned back round to see the woman still sitting on the same machine.

'Good afternoon,' he said to her as he walked out. She garbled something and watched him leave.

Harrison went straight to his room and into the shower. The run had helped, boosting his endorphins and giving him its own natural morphine effect. For now, it had also woken him up. A mental slap to get his act together. He was not going to let the Mannings win. He had a job to do and if they distracted him, he would be letting the victims down and potentially allowing the killer to strike again.

Harrison picked up his mobile phone and started looking through the missed calls and emails. There were three from the same number, he pressed call back.

'Bob Enson.' It was the rugby coach the lads from yesterday had suggested he speak to.

'Mr Enson, it's Dr Harrison Lane. I apologise for not being available to speak earlier.'

'Not a problem. I was keen to speak to you because I wanted to be sure you had the correct information. I'd like to see George's killer caught, but I'm not sure if it's related at all.'

'Please, just tell me the facts about what happened, Mr Enson.'

'George had recently joined the club as a fresher. He'd done well at his school, Harrow I think he was at, and said he was keen to keep it up. We were about five or six weeks into the term when he turned up for training but was obviously in pain. He went on the field, but he'd worn long Under Armour leggings underneath his shorts. He kept well out of the action and steered clear of any kind of contact with the rest of the team. Afterwards, it became clear why. He was covered in welts... the kind of bruising you get if you've been hit with a strap or long object of some kind. I mean, he was black and blue on his legs, buttocks and back. I asked him about it, and he said he'd fallen down the stairs. I can tell you there's no way those injuries were from a fall. To me, he looked like he had been beaten, but he refused to discuss it. I tried to talk to him about it a few times, and then he eventually stopped coming. We can't inform parents – the students are adults – but I always wondered what had gone on.'

'Was there any indication that he was a part of a secret society of any form?'

'I can't say I heard anything, but I was unlikely to. What I do know is that his attitude changed over those weeks he was with us. He started off as a diligent, polite, and pleasant lad. By the time he stopped coming, I was having serious thoughts about telling him to leave because he had become what I can only call elitist and, quite frankly, a prize shit. He called the other lads heathens, and seemed to think he was better than all of them. He wasn't good for the team.'

'Did you ever notice a tattoo on his hip?'

'No, but I'm not likely to have. I only saw the bruises because they were so obvious.'

Harrison thanked Bob and said he would ask one of the officers to get an official statement from him. This was critical evidence, because Harrison knew it was yet further clues to the fact George Marshwood had joined a secret association.

Once he'd read the email from Ryan, Harrison knew that his hunch from yesterday was right. The association was called the Moatside Monks. Ryan had found a deleted post on one of the student channels, mentioning the group and linking it to George. The post had been very quickly deleted, but he'd managed to grab a screenshot. Harrison needed to get into the station and share the latest findings with the team. He'd already lost valuable time thanks to his distraction with Freda Manning, and in investigations like this, time was critical.

The second he arrived, Lucy accosted him with a big, beaming smile. They'd received yet more sightings of the ghost monk. They were more random now, spread across the centre of the city. She showed him some of the new statements, jiggling around the desk like a cat on a hot tin roof.

'They're all pretty much the same. All said he had no face and disappeared without a trace. I was careful how I phrased any questions.'

He could tell she'd been working hard on her interview technique, but, nevertheless, most of the reports were pretty uniform, and none of them gave any further clues as to who it was, or what the ghost monk was doing.

'Most of them weren't caught on CCTV, but two of the witnesses got video footage on their phones.' Lucy had a trump card to show him after all. She paused a few moments, waiting for a reaction. 'This is the first time we've seen him on camera. It's proof he's real,' she added. 'The sightings are escalating, and the local paper has told us they've been sent a photograph of the ghost. They're going to email that over too.'

Harrison didn't share Lucy's enthusiasm because he suspected their 'ghost' had now become a potential money-spinning, viral social media opportunity, but he followed her to her desk where she had the clips up ready to show him.

The first was very short, but revealed a black-cloaked monk-like figure crossing one of the narrow, cobbled streets in Durham. He stood for a few moments and then disappeared up what seemed to be a small alley between some buildings.

'There were five witnesses to this,' Lucy said to Harrison.

He watched it again.

'Why does he stop in the middle of the street? It's as though he's making sure they've seen him,' Harrison said.

'This one is similar.' Lucy took control of the computer mouse and clicked on to the next video she wanted to show him. 'It's a few streets away, same night.'

Harrison watched as again the monk walked into the middle of the street. This time he had his hands clasped together as if in prayer. He stopped, lifted his head slightly, enough for the witnesses and the video viewers to see nothing but darkness under the hood, as though he had no face. Then he was gone.

'That's the best we've got so far. You can see what everyone is talking about. No face. It's creepy.'

'Mmhh,' Harrison replied.

'Yeah. I know what you're saying. It does look a bit, well... staged.'

'It does, but can you forward me the photo when it comes in from the paper?'

'Sure, of course,' Lucy replied. She looked disappointed that he didn't share her enthusiasm. 'Do you think they're genuine?' she asked him.

Harrison was just about to reply, when DS Urquhart marched up to them.

'Initial pathology results for Christopher are back from Dr Sharma, you might want to come and have a listen.'

Harrison thanked Lucy and they both followed the DS into the briefing room, where a small gathering of detectives was sitting expectantly in front of the large screen at the far end of the room. On the screen was Sunil's office. There was the sound of someone approaching, and Dr Sharma's cheerful face filled the screen. He was carrying a mug, and Harrison guessed he'd probably just been off to fill it up with his chai.

'Good afternoon, ladies and gentlemen,' he said. 'This will only be a short session, I fear, as you will appreciate you did not give me a lot to work with. Through dental records and DNA, we have identified our young man to be Christopher Downey. He was eighteen when he went missing. As he has been in the ground for a year, I am unable to say with 100 percent accuracy how he died, although I do have a good idea. There are no gunshot wounds or stab marks on the bones, and he was not poisoned like George. What I did find, however, are some fractures on his left femur and his sacrum in his lower back, consistent with blunt instrument trauma. Critically, the fracture on his femur could have been sufficient to kill him. I have seen injuries like this that have resulted in blood clots which have gone on to the heart or lungs, or if it severed the femoral artery, he would have bled to death rapidly. The femur is a tough bone – there was a fair amount of force needed to cause those fractures.'

'Are we talking a fall, or some kind of beating?' DI Steadman asked now. He'd come into the room and was stood at the back, arms and eyebrows crossed.

'In my view, these are not the kinds of injuries we would

expect to see from a fall. They are too localised. I would say he has been hit with something.'

'Dr Sharma, did you notice any healed blunt trauma injuries on George? I have spoken to witnesses who say that two years ago, when he was a fresher, he was covered in severe bruising on his thighs, buttocks and back which were consistent with being beaten.' Harrison asked.

'I was not looking for any fractures, but I remember seeing some scar tissue. Let me revisit that and get him scanned. I will get back to you as soon as I can.'

'Any more questions?' DI Steadman asked the room.

Everyone shook their heads.

'Thank you, Dr Sharma.'

'I would like to say a pleasure, but you know...' Sunil replied, nodding his head from side to side, and with a wry smile, he shut down the video feed.

DI Steadman turned to Harrison. 'Do you have any ideas about what we're dealing with here?'

'It fits in with the secret society theory,' Harrison began. 'I think it's hazing.'

A room of blank faces looked back at him. Steadman raised an eyebrow quizzically.

'Been around since medieval times. It's a brutal kind of initiation that was used to test new recruits or graduates and enforce respect for an organisation. It became popular among the US college fraternities, but they've really cracked down on it lately after students died or were permanently injured. You might also come across it sometimes in sports groups, the military and street gangs.'

'Hazing?'

'Yes, it can take several forms. One of the simplest methods is excessive alcohol bingeing; you're peer-pressured into drinking too much. Usually it just results in vomiting and an extremely bad hangover, but occasionally it goes too far and people are hospitalised. Among girls there's even a kind of mental torture option, whereby they body shame each other. The other form, which is the most popular among those associations that are all male, is beating or paddling the initiate. Plus sexual assaults are also used. It's a kind of dominance exercise, that the person joining is *owned* if you like, by that group, and if they take the torture, then they're loyal and make the grade to become a member.'

'So you're thinking that both Christopher and George joined this secret society, and to become a member they had to be beaten?'

'Yes.'

'Why would they allow that, and who would do it? These are not supposed to be stupid people, they're meant to be some of the country's most intelligent students. George and Christopher came from wealthy families, they didn't need for anything.'

'It would be the existing members who would do the beating, and they'd suffer it because the society offered them a brotherhood, a sense of belonging and a support network.'

'Bloody idiots if you ask me.'

Harrison didn't reply. He didn't need to.

'So, say Christopher took part in this hazing ritual. It wasn't intended to kill him, just test him?'

Harrison nodded.

'So his death could have been an accident and would almost certainly involve the whole group, not just one individual. Would also explain the different presentations of the two bodies. Christopher's was hidden, and an attempt made to hide forensic evidence, while George was very public and clearly intentional.'

'Indeed, so you have the possibility of a leaky boat in relation to Christopher's death. Perhaps one of the group struggled with their secret.'

'Perhaps George was the weak link?'

'Perhaps. I also think I know the name of their group. I found some symbols yesterday, which I think are connected, graffitied on some walls in Moatside Lane. Plus, my technical analyst managed to capture a post on one of the student chat boards, which mentions the Moatside Monks in relation to George.'

'Moatside? That's where George lived with the other lads.'

DI Steadman and DS Urquhart exchanged glances.

'Told you that lot were hiding something. No wonder they've got the best lawyers on hand,' Steadman said. 'Can you brief the forensics photographer? We're going to need every little morsel of evidence we can get. Why haven't we heard about this group? Why doesn't anyone come forward?'

'Fear, misplaced loyalty. Perhaps those who know about it enjoy the fact they're in the know and the rest of the world isn't. But, I'd say the reason that post got taken down so fast is because they're scared,' Harrison replied.

'But that still doesn't explain the phantom ghost monk. What are they up to?' Urquhart asked Harrison. 'Was it George, and now it's another member of the group?'

'It could have been George. It has to be someone who knew that Christopher was killed and therefore that would suggest it's one of the group, or someone close to them. I think the recent sightings are copycats or just a form of mass hysteria. Once Christopher was found, I think our original monk retired.'

'Or was killed.'

'Indeed.'

'Bloody ghost, my arse,' Steadman said, gritting his teeth. 'He's a right pain in the proverbial. Thanks to him it seems like we've got every bloody media outlet in the world here, and sightings are coming in every day, tying up our resources. Right, we need to focus on those five lads. There has to be another weak link somewhere. I also want a team questioning everyone at the college about these so-called Moatside Monks. If it exists, then some of them will have heard about it and might talk. We've no idea how many members are in the group. Perhaps one of them has left. And get hold of university authorities. If this hazing business is going on, they need to know so they can be on top of it.'

The meeting broke up, but just as Harrison was about to leave, David Urquhart came up to him.

'We've got Annabelle, the girlfriend of Christopher Downey, coming in to the Durham city police station for a chat. Do you want to tag along? She was interviewed when he went missing, but with this recent development we need to talk to her again and get a statement. Perhaps she might be able to throw some light on what went on and possibly confirm he was involved with the Moatside Monks.'

18

Ryan was impeccable with his timing, as always. He'd been running a facial recognition programme across social media. Given the amount of images, it invariably took a while, but he'd found two very interesting posts. Neither of them were from any of the people linked to their inquiry, but someone had accidentally captured them in the background of other photographs.

The first was in the Undercroft Bar at University College in the Castle. Two girls had taken a selfie, but not framed it well, probably because they both looked like they'd been to a happy hour which had stretched on longer than sixty minutes. In the background was a group of male students sitting together. Christopher Downey was sitting next to Mark Lloyd-Jones and David Alexander, two of the other lads from George Marshwood's house in Moatside. They were all laughing and smiling, relaxed in each other's company. It was three days before Christopher disappeared. The second image was outside; a shot of Palace Green and walking together, deep in conversation, were Christopher and Mark.

'Excellent. How the hell did he find these?' DI Steadman asked when Harrison showed him.

'Ryan uses software that most forces have available, but adds a few extras of his own. I don't pretend to know what it is, but it works.'

'We know that Mark and Christopher went to the same school, which, incidentally, Annabelle went to. This helps prove a solid link between him and the Moatside gang. Let's put this all to Ms Keyes and see what she has to say.'

THE DURHAM POLICE station was on New Elvet, not far across the river from Harrison's hotel. The white building could have been just another old house, apart from the access ramp to the entrance, and blue police lamp hanging outside.

Annabelle Keyes was a slim – verging on too slim, sporty young woman – with pale skin, and Harrison could clearly see she was anxious. The skin around her fingernails was pink and red where she'd bitten her fingertips.

'Thank you for coming in, Miss Keyes. I'm DS David Urquhart and this is DC Emily Mitchell. Observing is Dr Harrison Lane, who is helping us with this inquiry. Dr Lane is trying to build up a profile of the person who killed George Marshwood and we are also looking into whether Christopher may have been one of his victims.'

Annabelle nodded jerkily, the nerves coming out in her movements.

'Firstly, we just wanted to give our condolences. I know Christopher has been missing for a year, but the news must have come as a shock to you.'

'Yes, it was,' she replied quietly. 'I'm just relieved that he's been discovered.'

Nerves aside, Harrison didn't think that it had been a shock at all. Annabelle was all contradictions. She said yes, but her body and voice said no. She did look as though she might burst into tears at any point, but was that because of Christopher, or for a more selfish reason? She'd also used the word 'discovered', which seemed an odd choice to him. 'Found' would have been a more appropriate word.

Before he'd come to the interview, Harrison had read her original statement from the missing persons inquiry. To him there was a distinct lack of urgency in her words, as though she knew there was no point in the police trying to find him. What he'd seen and read already suggested to him that Annabelle Keyes knew her boyfriend had been killed. Question was, why and by whom? And why hadn't she spoken out before?

'Would you like to tell us in your own words how you knew Christopher?'

'We were at school together, Charterhouse, and had been going out for two years before we came to Durham. He was a lovely guy.'

'I know it's a year ago now, but can you take us back to the days before Christopher disappeared? What was he doing, who was he seeing?'

'I told the other police all this,' she said. 'We didn't always see each other every day because of lectures and stuff, plus we didn't want to crowd each other at uni. I'd seen him the day before. He was fine.'

'Who were his friends?'

Annabelle shrugged, and Harrison noticed her jaw tighten as she clenched her teeth. Again, contradictory indications. The question clearly stressed her, but she was behaving as though she didn't know, and it didn't matter.

'No one in particular. We saw a few friends from school, and Chris's roomie and he often went out.'

'Roommate, that's Luke Thomason?'

'Yes.'

'And school friends, did that include Mark Lloyd-Jones?'

Annabelle blinked and paused.

'I think he bumped into him around college a couple of times.'

She blinked again and seemed to hold her breath.

'We have two photographs of Christopher and Mark together. They looked quite friendly. More than just bumping into each other.'

Annabelle stared at the two printouts of the images Ryan had sent through. She shook her head. 'I wasn't there.'

'Did Christopher seem upset or anxious about anything in the days before he went missing?'

'No.'

She said it with conviction. Harrison saw her breath again. This question didn't stress her like the previous ones. So Christopher hadn't been expecting what had happened.

'Did Christopher join, or want to join any societies or perhaps even secret clubs?'

Annabelle clasped her arms around her body as though giving herself a hug. She clearly found this question distressing, and her emotions showed in the tenseness of her jaw and mouth.

'I don't think so.'

'Did he have any enemies, someone who may have threatened him.'

'No.'

Again, a firm *no*, much more convincing than her reply to his previous question. If Christopher wasn't killed by an enemy, then it strongly suggested it had been a so-called friend, or even girlfriend, who'd been responsible for his demise – accidentally or not.

They got little more out of the interview. Harrison watched Annabelle leave.

'What do we know about Annabelle Keyes?' He asked DS Urquhart.

Urquhart looked up from his notes. 'Nothing flagged up on her records. She comes from a stable family background, did well at school and has always kept her nose clean. She used to be a gymnast for her county, won a lot of awards and nearly went to the Olympics by all accounts. That must have taken a lot of focus and clean living to keep that up.'

'Gymnast? Then she would be agile,' Harrison said, as much to himself as the detective.

'Agile? Well, yeah, I guess so. They jump around and do somersaults and stuff. Not my sport, but I've seen it on the TV when the Olympics have been on.'

AFTER THE INTERVIEW WITH ANNABELLE, the tiredness came back in a tsunami and Harrison returned to his hotel for an early dinner and bed. He ate in the hotel restaurant, choosing to sit by the big windows where he was able to look out over the river. Despite the exercise earlier, he wasn't massively hungry. Tiredness was often an appetite killer and his stomach was still struggling to find some after the emotional morning. In the end he chose a Thai fish curry which was tasty and not too heavy.

The waitress was a thirty-something Asian woman who had dyed her hair bright pink, and her personality matched her hair. She was bright and cheerful and a real antidote to his day. Although Harrison didn't usually strike up conversations with strangers, he managed to glean a potted version of her life story before he'd even finished his main course. She, however, learned nothing about him other than that he was polite and a good listener.

While he ate, he texted Tanya to test the waters and see if she was still annoyed with him. He felt guilty about his lack of attention to her. She deserved better.

It wasn't as if he didn't want to see her. There were times he could feel the ache inside when he thought about her, or looked at a photograph, but he couldn't compromise his work. It was everything to him. If he was honest, it wasn't just work that kept him at arm's length; it was also the Mannings and the dark shadows in his head. He wondered if she would get tired of him. He wouldn't blame her.

Dinner eaten, Harrison headed up to his room. A full belly made him feel even more exhausted, and he had an image of the bed that awaited him, imprinted on his mind.

Tanya replied saying she was up to her eyes at a big value break-in and would speak to him tomorrow. An hour later, Jack also checked in on Harrison, obviously concerned about how the morning's meeting had affected him. Harrison texted back that he was fine.

Harrison was fine as long as he kept his eyes open, but each time he closed them, Freda Manning's face wormed its way back into his head and floated across his eyelids. He was desperate for sleep. His nerves were jangling through tiredness so he turned on some classical music to purge the memories from his tired brain. It took another hour before his head and body stopped struggling to escape, and he slipped into sleep.

19

The emotional and physical exhaustion meant that when Harrison awoke to the sound of his mobile phone ringing at 8 a.m. the next morning, he opened his eyes with his heart racing – not knowing where he was momentarily, or why he was there. It took just seconds to adjust, but it felt like he was dragging himself out of a long, dark tunnel towards the light.

DS David Urquhart's voice pulled his conscious back into reality.

'We've arrested the ghost monk,' he said. 'Extra patrols last night finally managed to trap him. He's due to be interviewed in around an hour in Durham. Do you want to be there?'

'Absolutely. I'll be in.'

Harrison jumped in the shower, alternating the water from hot to cold to shock his body into re-starting. He felt like somebody had taken one of those strawberry or apple corers and stuck it right into his guts so that there was an empty, painful hole in his centre. It made him so angry that the

Mannings were still able to do this to him. He'd tried hard to take back control of his life and emotions, and yet just the mention of their name made his stomach churn.

He skipped breakfast and went straight to the station to hunt down DS Urquhart and their phantom monk. This could be the breakthrough in the case they had been waiting for.

David and DC Emily Mitchell were preparing to go in.

'So, any thoughts on how you feel we should handle this, or what you'd like answered?' he asked Harrison.

'Who is it?'

'It's a Martin Jones. He's a student at Collingwood. Told the arresting officers he was just doing it for a laugh and he's got nothing to do with the murders.'

'Mmhh,' Harrison replied.

Urquhart and Mitchell were both sat watching his face, waiting for Harrison's guidance.

'You go ahead with the interview but I have a suspicion he's telling the truth.'

Both of the detectives exchanged eyebrow raises. They hadn't been expecting that.

WHILE HARRISON WAITED to be told which room to go into, DI Steadman arrived, his face all creases.

'Bloody phantom monk is causing us no end of headaches. There were another fifteen reports in first thing this morning. I'm thinking copycats and nothing to do with our case. You?'

The musky scent of Steadman's aftershave enveloped Harrison, and he noticed that the DI was looking a little smarter than he'd seen him in previous days. It looked like he'd used some kind of product on his black hair, which was now slick and lustrous, and a tie poked out from his jacket pocket.

Harrison nodded.

'Do you think the original ghost monk is even out there still? It could have been George.'

'Maybe. Maybe not. I think there was a purpose to the appearances originally, to do with Christopher. Now the sightings are random and these,' he nodded to the board, 'are definitely looking like whoever it is wants to be seen. Could be a member of the Moathouse Monks in amongst the sightings, but definitely at least some, if not all now, are copycats.'

'We're verging on mass hysteria out there. I'm having to do a press briefing later and I could really do with some good progress. International TV crews have arrived to cover the story. We're making headlines in the States and Canada, and even Australia. I need to get this sewn up and a lid put on our phantom. Worst possible combination; a ghost story in a city full of students who love nothing more than to prank each other. If we're not careful, someone is going to get injured. The locals aren't always as humoured by their jokes as their fellow students. You watching the interview?'

Harrison nodded again.

'I'll join you. I've got to think of what to say at the press conference. I've a meeting with the media team at headquarters in around an hour, and they're hounding me every minute of the day for some progress.'

MARTIN JONES TURNED out to be a Geography student from Surrey who looked like he was about to face a firing squad and would burst into tears if anyone said *boo* to him.

'Don't think he thought this one through, do you?' DI Steadman sighed next to Harrison. They were watching via video in a viewing room next door to the interview suite. Even from the other room, they could smell the fear.

'I suspect not,' Harrison replied.

'In your own words, would you tell us what you were doing last night dressed as a monk on Bow Lane?' DS Urquhart said to Martin in the interview room.

The young lad's eyes widened, and he launched straight in.

'It was a dare, a joke. I didn't mean it to get serious. Everyone's been talking about the ghost monk. Some of the girls were going into town and they'd been winding themselves up in case the ghost appeared. A few of us thought it would be a laugh to scare them and then film it. We were going to freak them out and then go and rescue them. Thought one of the TV crews might be around, too. Give them something to talk about.' Martin looked incredibly sheepish and looked down at his lap. 'I know, not exactly PC, but it was just a bit of fun. I didn't hurt anyone or anything.' His eyes welled with tears.

'We?'

'Myself and two friends from college.'

'Are you a member of any societies?'

'Societies? Err, yeah, I'm in the Curry Club and the Craft Beer Society.'

'Any secret societies?'

'No.'

'Did you know George Marshwood?'

Martin shook his head so violently he looked like something out of the exorcist.

'No. Never met him. I swear I've got nothing to do with his

murder. I don't know anything about it. I wouldn't joke about that.'

'What about Christopher Downey?'

His name had the same effect.

'They're both University College, and not in my faculty either. Never met them.'

'Are you aware of any secret societies that exist in Durham?'

'Secret societies?'

'Yes.'

Martin shrugged and thought for a moment. 'I don't know any that are secret. There's sort of semi-secret ones that everyone has heard of like the Hatfield Cavaliers, The Exiles and the Castle Fives, but I think they're like dining clubs for the rich public-school crowd. That's all. I guess if they're secret, I wouldn't know about them.'

'Have you dressed up as the ghost monk any other night besides last night?'

'No. Honestly, you can ask my mates. It was just last night.'

Harrison turned to DI Steadman. 'He's definitely not the original ghost monk. I think your problem is there are a whole load of Martins out there who are causing a state of hysteria just to have a laugh. The original monk has gone to ground, because I think their purpose has been achieved.'

'Murder?'

'Maybe, maybe not. If we work on the idea that Christopher's death was an accident. The hazing got out of control, then there were several people who knew about his death and who were party to the disposal of his body. Maybe one of them wasn't happy about it, but for whatever reason couldn't report it. Perhaps it was this person who visited his burial site because they knew eventually someone would take notice – and maybe they also wanted to spook the others.'

'What about George?'

'The original ghost monk could have been George. I don't think so though. Analysing the witness statements, I think they were still active the day after George died. It could be that the monk killed George in revenge for Christopher's death, or that they were simply drawing attention to it. Until we find out the members of that group, then we are going to have to keep on guessing. We need to focus on the house in Moatside. Try to get a search warrant.'

'A lot easier said than done. The lawyers will resist any attempt to look at those lads. I need some strong evidence to get a warrant.'

'Then we have to find something and get clever about it.'

'OK, I'm going to find every past girlfriend they've had in the last two years and ask them if they have a tattoo on their hip. If we can get proof of a secret society, then we can really start to go to town. Right now though, I'm going to solve our phantom monk epidemic and hold a press conference. It's Martin's lucky day. We can cut him a deal, no charges, but he needs to tell the world that the ghost monk has been caught and end this now. He will get his day in the limelight and we'll get some peace to focus on our murder inquiry.'

THERE HAD BEEN one loose end in Harrison's jigsaw of clues, and that related to what the rugby lads had said about the ghost simply disappearing when they'd given chase. He went back to the incident room and asked for CCTV covering the whole of Durham city centre that night after George's murder. He knew nobody in a monk's cloak had been caught on camera, but maybe they'd already ditched the cloak. There was one face in particular he was looking for.

It took him two hours, and two large mugs of green tea, but he found it. It was a camera on North Bailey that captured her. She'd obviously ditched the cloak and mask before she got to the street, but even from the grainy image, he could tell she looked flustered. As she got onto the street, she smoothed down her hair and looked around her, no doubt worried that the lads might have made their way there too. A few moments later, they did indeed appear jogging down the road, clearly still looking for where their phantom could have reappeared. She turned and looked in a shop window and they jogged straight past. Then Annabelle Keyes carried on walking past Hatfield College and towards Saddler Street.

Harrison sat back, closed his eyes, and let his brain do some thinking.

20

By lunchtime, the team had three women who all said that they'd seen the tattoo of the double M on James Althrop, Oscar Whittington, and Mark Lloyd-Jones. That was three out of the five in the house. In addition, they had a male student come forward who had been to a beach party a couple of weeks before, which had been held by the Moatside Monks to choose their next members. Needless to say, this student hadn't been chosen, and while he was keen that nobody knew it was him talking to the police, his sour grapes at being rejected worked in their favour. The net was closing, and DI John Steadman was keen to pull it tighter. He called the core team together for a quick tactical meeting. Seven of them sat around the meeting room table, including Harrison, David Urquhart and Emily Mitchell.

'I want to pull them all in,' DI Steadman said. He had a pen in his hand and as he talked, he spun it around his fingers, the adrenaline coursing through his body as he finally began to smell blood in their hunt. 'We need to start rattling their cages and seeing what we can shake out. Their lawyers are going to keep them tight-lipped. I'm expecting "no comment" all the way, so any suggestions Harrison as to how we break through?'

'I want to see them together, just the lads on their own. Look at the group dynamics. That should tell us who are the weaker players and who is calling the shots. Then we can target them more effectively and dig deeper.'

'Yes, good idea. There has to be a ringleader and it makes sense to separate them so we can pick off the weaker ones. That won't be easy. They each come with a lawyer, but I'm sure we can call them all in together and then come up with an excuse to give the lawyers a briefing so we can view the boys alone. Leave that to me. We won't obviously be able to question them without their briefs. Any ideas as to how to stir up the happy family?'

'We need a catalyst, something that is going to get them scared. Think about turning on each other. An image of the tattoo might do it. If they've all got them, then it's evidence they're linked and that might panic them. You could perhaps accidentally drop the papers or just allow them to see it. Wouldn't you be disclosing that to the lawyers, anyway? Tell them you want their clients to voluntarily disclose if they have one or not.'

'I think that can all be arranged.' Steadman smiled and rubbed his hands together. He was clearly relishing the upcoming battle. 'Harrison, we can watch. David and Emily, you run the interviews as before.'

DI STEADMAN and his team succeeded in arranging for all five of the Moatside students to come into the Durham station and 'help with enquiries' later that afternoon. They were reluctant, but the lawyers all agreed, probably because they wanted to know what the police had and how to proceed with defending their clients. Not to mention the prospect of racking up a nice meaty invoice.

The five students were shown into a large interview suite, where they all sat with their own briefs, waiting to be called in. Harrison and DI Steadman were watching them next door.

All of the lads carried the air of money about them, a confidence and grooming that said they could always have the best. They were dressed, as only rich people could, to look casual but dripping with top-notch brands that would have cost a fortune. Their attire was a long way from the majority of Primark and ASOS-clad students who walked the streets of Durham and other university corridors.

'They don't look too worried, do they?' Steadman commented. The lads were lounging on the chairs, looking as if they were waiting for a train, not to be interviewed as part of a murder inquiry. 'Let's hope David can wipe the smirks off their faces.'

Right on cue, DS Urquhart walked into the room and proceeded to ask the lawyers if they could come with him to another room for a quick briefing. As he talked, he placed his folder of notes down on the table in the middle of the room. An image of the tattoo was clear for everyone to see. All the lads' eyes were drawn to it, and the atmosphere in the room noticeably changed. Those with suits on followed Urquhart out of the room, and he picked up his folder on the way, holding the picture outermost to ensure everyone had seen it.

As soon as the door was shut, two of the lads turned to the others.

'Did you see the tattoo?' one of them whispered.

'That's James Althrop,' Steadman said to Harrison.

He was a good-looking young man with black hair and a healthy suntan. Dressed in a Berluti branded hoody with black chinos, his whole outfit would have probably set his parents back by at least £1,000. Harrison wrote a note next to his name.

'They don't know what it means, we can just say it's a friendship thing.'

'David Alexander,' Steadman identified him to Harrison.

Being good-looking appeared to be a prerequisite for this group. Harrison wouldn't call any of them plain, apart from the one who sat slightly apart from the others in the corner.

'David's father is a retail billionaire, minor member of the nobility, but invested well and obviously has a good business head. He married a supermodel. He's their only child so set to inherit a fortune.' John added.

Harrison mused that money attracted good looks and even if one parent hadn't fared so well in those stakes, the other would be more likely to be stunning. David was the best-looking of them all. He gave the impression he'd just dropped by from a film set. Blonde hair and bright-blue eyes and an athletic body. All of these lads had a lot to lose if they were found guilty of murder. No wonder the parents had brought in the big gun lawyers.

'Shut it. It *is* a friendship mark.' The brown-haired lad in the corner hissed to them all in an American accent. He glared at each one, raising his eyebrows and making it obvious that walls might have ears.

'And that is Joseph Goode. The dad's some kind of porn film mogul. Made his fortune making trashy videos in the days when videos were a thing and streaming was when you had a runny nose as a kid!'

'Should we come up with something so we can say what it stands for if they ask?' James asked Joseph, tentatively.

'No, just say "no comment" like we've been told,' he whispered back, barely audible.

They all went quiet.

Harrison watched their faces closely. There were a few glances towards Joseph, with just the occasional furtive look at each other. He stayed in the same relaxed pose, almost ignoring them while they waited for their lawyers to return.

'Well, that wasn't too exciting, but it seemed to confirm what we suspected. What do you think Harrison?'

'Joseph Goode is obviously the ringleader, and we should concentrate on James Althrop as the weakest link. I'd definitely like to know a lot more about Mr Goode and his background.'

'Let's see how the interviews go. I'd like to try to hold them here as long as possible, see if we can rattle them some more.'

THE FIRST CROSS-EXAMINATION was with Oscar Whittington, who sat next to his suited lawyer in the interview room with the air of someone who was going to be untouchable. His hair was dead straight, and he had a lopsided fringe which kept falling over his left eye, causing him to make a very irritating flick of his head.

The interview started in an unremarkable way, as they are apt to. Oscar gave his name and confirmed that he was a housemate of the recently deceased George. At the mention of George's name, emotion for his friend momentarily overtook Oscar's selfish survival instincts. It seemed genuine, but

Harrison also detected a slight undercurrent of something else. An element of fear.

When DC Emily Mitchell asked him to tell her what happened on the day of the murder, Oscar launched into his well-rehearsed story. Harrison could tell it was rehearsed for several reasons. Firstly, he paused far too often as his mind clearly tried to remember what it was he should say, choosing his words carefully rather than simply recounting a memory. Oscar also watched the detectives' faces closely, searching for signs that they were believing him, or that he hadn't said something which contradicted with his previous statement or that by one of the others. His story was also completely in sequence. He didn't jump around; it was one time point after another. When he'd recounted the entire day, ending with George saying he was going out for a walk to meet a friend, it was with relief, as though he'd managed to recite a memorised poem at an oral exam.

Then the questions began, and his body language shifted. Now he was going to have to think on his feet, and he became defensive. His arms moved to lock across his chest, and he started to swallow harder. It was also at this point that he started to throw glances at his lawyer, which seemed to be for support, and to double-check that the latest lie had passed the test.

When the interviewer asked Oscar if he knew who George had met, there was no doubt in Harrison's mind that he was lying.

'No, no I don't. Absolutely not,' Oscar replied. His voice dropped in volume. Shortly after, Harrison saw him rub his nose. His blood pressure had risen, causing the capillaries in his nostrils to swell and itch. Oscar was lying. There was no doubt about that. The question was why, and who was he protecting? Himself or someone else?

The next three interviews went pretty much along the same lines. James Althrop, Mark Lloyd-Jones and David Alexander all repeated the same story, pretty much word for word. They'd got up. Everyone had been fine. Most of them went out to various different departments and lecture halls, and then they all came home for dinner. They ate together and afterwards, George said he was going out for a walk and had arranged to meet a friend. When it came to the questioning, they too showed subtle signs of stress. They had to all be in on the lie. That meant the five might not only have colluded in hiding Christopher's death, but now they were colluding in murder.

DS Urquhart had asked both Mark and David about Christopher. When he showed David the two photographs of them talking, there had been a visible shiver run across the student's face. He clearly hadn't been expecting that. He regained his composure quickly however, told Urquhart that they were at school together so had occasionally bumped into each other, and any other questions after that he just shrugged and said he didn't know.

It was the final interview that Harrison found the most interesting. Joseph Goode, the American student. There was an extra air of confidence about him. He leaned back in the chair and put his arms behind his head. It was a relaxed pose, opening up his body and showing that he wasn't scared of anything. He repeated the same story as the others, but there were a couple of subtle differences.

At the first mention of George, Harrison watched Joseph's face closely. Where the others had showed signs of grief, Joseph's reaction was fake. Instead of his eyebrows being raised and the corners of his mouth going down, Joseph's eyebrows also went down and his mouth went into some kind of a pout. It was like a child who had done something wrong and was now trying to look contrite in front of their parents, without feeling any real remorse.

The other sign for Harrison, was the fact Joseph never once mentioned George by name. It was always 'he' or 'him'. He had distanced himself from George psychologically.

When DS Urquhart questioned him about the tattoo, Joseph Goode stuck to the script.

'Would you mind if I went in and asked some questions?' Harrison turned to Steadman.

'No, be my guest. Make him squirm, won't you!'

Harrison walked next door. He saw the suspicion on Joseph's face when he entered and knew he had a few moments of the upper hand while the student worked him out.

'Dr Lane is a psychologist working with us,' said DS Urquhart. 'He has a few additional questions.'

Harrison sat down and put his elbows onto the table so that he could draw his upper body up straight. He wanted to be physically dominating to see what effect that had on Joseph.

'So, Joseph, you have a little secret association going on. Tell me how that came about?'

Joseph glared back at him, pausing before speaking. 'It's just a friendship group, that's all.'

'But two of your friendship group are dead.'

'Two?'

'Yes, we know there are links between the group and Christopher Downey who went missing a year ago. I'm sure you're aware that we have recently recovered his remains.'

Joseph didn't bat an eyelid. 'What kind of links, Dr Lane?'

He hadn't taken long to regain his composure and wasn't intimidated. He clearly thought he could hit it straight back to Harrison.

'We have photographs of Christopher socialising with Mark and David.'

'He was in our college and he went to school with Mark. They were bound to hook up now and then. What are you implying, Dr Lane?'

Harrison went down another route, unfazed. 'You dropped out of college in the US, didn't you?'

Joseph shrugged. 'You obviously know I did. Didn't like the course.'

'Did you want to start your own Skull and Bones society? Couldn't get into the real thing at Yale so thought you'd start your own here?' Harrison asked Joseph.

'Be real, Dr Lane. The Skull and Bones society is not far off two hundred years old and has its own properties. Do you really think our little dinner parties are on the same scale?'

'I think you wanted the same effect. The brotherhood, the secrecy, the opportunity to get away with anti-social behaviour all in the name of your little group.' Harrison emphasised the word little.

'That's a lot of,' Joseph turned to his lawyer, 'what do you call it? Ah yes, conjecture, or should I say, guesswork.' He turned back to Harrison and glared at him defiantly.

Harrison did the same into Joseph Goode's eyes. He could see the anger smouldering in them because he'd challenged him. Yet they still said that he thought he was untouchable. Harrison went for the topic he suspected might be Joseph's Achilles heel.

'You know, what I don't get is that all the rest of the lads in the house are all linked to British nobility, they're from the privileged class, old money. Then there's you. The odd one out. How did you get invited into that group?'

Harrison watched the twitch on Joseph Goode's smug face. He'd hit a bullseye. That clearly struck home.

'I'm not going to even bother answering that question.'

Harrison smiled. 'Thank you, I got my answer.'

Joseph's face tightened, and he pulled his lips tight to keep his control. Then he leaned back in his chair and crossed his arms defiantly as he watched Harrison leave the room.

'SMUG BASTARD, isn't he? But I think you rang his bell towards the end.' DI Steadman smirked at Harrison as he returned to the viewing room. 'I think from what we've seen, they're definitely hiding something. Now we have to find out if they're all involved in both deaths. I'm not going to let them get off scot free. What's the Skull and Bones Society?'

'It's the oldest secret society at Yale University. Said to count some of the most powerful people in America amongst its members. Been going since the 1800s and has its own property, called the Tomb, and its own Island retreat. Former presidents have been members, and other very senior politicians and powerful businessmen. Lots of conspiracy theories around its membership and what goes on at ceremonies.'

'There's a whole other world out there I never even knew existed.'

'Indeed, but you can be sure that Joseph Goode would not have been invited to join it.'

Harrison's phone buzzed in his pocket. He'd been expecting a text from Ryan.

'I think we might have something. My colleague has just told me that six months after Joseph Goode left the American college he'd been studying at before Durham, the college received a very large donation. Ralph Goode, Joseph's father, was the donor.' Harrison looked up from his phone. 'Why give a very large donation to somewhere that your son didn't enjoy and didn't even finish his degree at?'

'We spoke to them. They said he left because the course wasn't the right fit for him. There was no evidence of a scandal.'

'Then I find that very peculiar. Why would his father pay a very large donation to the university after Joseph left? If you give donations it's to say thank you for something, surely?'

'You're right, it sounds like a pay-off. I'll get on to it straight away. Someone must know what was behind it. In the meantime we'll think of something to keep them here to stew a bit. I'm sure the lawyers will be quite happy racking up their hourly fees while they hang around.'

Harrison put Joseph Goode at the top of his suspect list and told Ryan to keep digging. He decided to go through the CCTV again from the night that George was killed, just in case he spotted Joseph sneaking down to the riverside. Everyone on the team was feverishly working to find that one extra clue which could give them the upper hand in the investigation. All eyes kept looking at the clock. It was just a matter of time before the Moatside mob and their lawyers walked out.

Harrison was getting nowhere with the CCTV, which didn't surprise him. Joseph wasn't a fool. He'd have covered his tracks if he had killed George.

'We've just heard back from Dr Sharma,' John announced to the team, 'George had some evidence of trauma to his thigh and buttocks area. Nothing as severe as he found on Christopher, but he would be able to confidently say that George had at some point in the last couple of years been hit several times, or beaten.'

That news spurred everyone on. The evidence was mounting.

DI Steadman paced up and down the incident room. They were close to making a breakthrough, and he had the paperwork ready to submit for a search warrant. He just needed something else to give them enough grounds to search Moatside and to use as leverage with the weaker members of the group. They'd already heard from all the lawyers that their clients declined the invitation to show if they had a tattoo on their hips. That hadn't been a surprise.

Suddenly, DS Urquhart slammed down the phone and jumped up triumphantly. 'Yes!' He said punching the air. 'We've got him. The president of Joseph Goode's college wouldn't say a word, said the matter was all sorted, but I spoke to a local news journalist who was delighted to talk to me. She'd been disgusted at what had gone on. Joseph was accused of hazing and bullying in the fraternity house he belonged to. The college kept it out of police hands and his father paid off the lad Joseph had beaten, and made the donation to the college. She described him as a sadistic bully who was obsessed with feelings of inferiority because of where his dad had come from and where their money was made. Cost the dad a fortune to keep it out the papers and pay everyone off. Her paper wouldn't run with the story because his lawyers were all over them and would have tied them up in court for years. If they hadn't bankrupted them first. She's emailing me over some information.' He positively beamed with the news and it instantly lifted the mood of the entire incident room.

'Excellent,' said Steadman, a huge smile breaking the frown which had been rooted on his features all day. 'Now we have a good reason to keep Joseph in. Separate him from the others and see if we can weaken his influence. They might speak out if he's not such a threat. Go and tell him the good news, David and let's see if we can get anything else on him for this warrant.'

21

Harrison still had one loose end to tie up. Someone who could throw more light on what had gone on and help determine who had been responsible for George's death. The ghost monk.

She didn't sound too keen on the phone, but Annabelle Keyes agreed to see him and he left the incident room for her university accommodation off Owengate.

On his way, Harrison thought about how he should approach their conversation. It was still a possibility that she had murdered George in a revenge killing. They now knew it was a poisoning, but the other injuries – especially the triangular piece of skin that had been cut and the symbols on his torso – all pointed to a sadistic killer. From what Harrison had seen, that certainly didn't describe Annabelle. He'd contemplated telling DS David Urquhart or DI John Steadman where he was going and getting one of them to come with him, but he knew that would terrify her. If he had any hope of getting to the truth of what had gone on the night

Christopher died, then this needed to be an unofficial chat before he asked her to go on the record.

Annabelle looked decidedly unsure as she opened the door to Harrison. If he'd thought she looked nervous at the police station, the anxiety had ramped up to full throttle. Her neck was red and her hands shook slightly as she showed him into her room.

He tried to put her at ease, but they both knew the conversation wasn't going to be an easy one.

Annabelle offered him the only chair and sat herself on her bed. It was a neat room, small and packed with her personality. On the walls were photographs of her and Christopher, laughing, holding hands, pulling silly faces as selfies. Plus, there were a couple of her in her gymnastic heyday, a particularly good image of her somersaulting off a horse, and another of her receiving a very large cup. On her desk was a family photograph. Annabelle and her parents, with what Harrison assumed to be her younger sister and their dog, a big yellow Labrador whose tongue took up half the photograph.

'Have you stopped the gymnastics?' Harrison asked, nodding at the two photographs.

Annabelle looked over at them.

'Yeah, pretty much. I'm too old now really and you've got to practise so much to keep on top of your fitness that it's just not practical to carry on here.'

'You're still fit and agile, though,' Harrison looked at her now.

It was clear Annabelle wasn't stupid. She immediately knew the hidden meaning behind that statement, and she looked away, biting her bottom lip.

'You see that map...' She nodded at a printout of the map

of the world with dozens of tiny crosses on it. 'Chris and I were planning to travel after uni. We had it all worked out.'

'Don't you want to see his killer brought to justice?'

'Of course I do.'

'Then why don't you talk to us?'

'Things aren't straightforward.'

'I need to know a couple of crucial pieces of information which could ensure Joseph Goode doesn't get away.'

Annabelle had looked up, shocked when he said Joseph's name.

'Was he the ringleader responsible for Christopher's death, even if he wasn't entirely to blame?'

'I can't...' Annabelle's face showed the enormous emotional struggle she was trying to wrestle.

'I'm not here to take an official statement. For now, this is an informal chat. I'm a psychologist, not a detective. This is between you and me.'

Harrison let that sink in for a few moments. He could tell she was struggling with the urge to speak out, but something was holding her back. He tried to goad it out of her.

'What about George? Did you kill George because of what he did to Christopher?'

Annabelle looked up, shocked.

'No. No way, I couldn't kill anyone. George was struggling with it all. Found it difficult to keep up the lies. He came to me, all repentant and crying, about two weeks before he died, but they were crocodile tears. He was just scared of being caught. Wanted to blame it all on Joseph, but he was frightened of him. They all are. I asked him to leave. He didn't really care about Christopher.'

'Joseph is currently at the police station being questioned. I'd like to ensure he stays there.'

Annabelle looked up again and searched Harrison's face. She gave the tiniest of nods. He took that as a tentative yes to proceed.

'How did you know where they'd buried him?'

She looked down again. Her chin creased, and her bottom lip trembled.

Harrison waited.

'I was there.'

He instantly had questions he wanted to ask, but he held back. Let her tell her story in her own time.

'I went with him that night to the selection dinner in Moatside. He was so excited. I don't drink much, never have because it just wasn't an option with the gymnastics. They plied us with alcohol, told me I was drinking fruit juice, but it wasn't. There were only a couple of other girls there, and they did the same to them. They egged Christopher on to drink more and more. Made it into some kind of macho competition. He really wanted to be a part of the group. It was supposed to be so prestigious. Mark Lloyd-Jones had sold it to him. Said they were going to have influence in all the highest places. They were building a network which would help each other out, and the rest of the time they would enjoy the best things in life. It was only for the chosen few. Christopher had been chosen, and he wanted to prove himself.'

Annabelle stopped for a moment, and a shiver ran through her body. She looked young and fragile on the bed.

'Then Joseph said that he had to undergo an initiation and so did I if I was to be the girlfriend of a Moatside Monk. They separated us. Put me in another room, but I was comatose by then. I lay down on a bed and that was it, just passed out. I'm not sure if it was just alcohol, or if there had also been drugs in my drink, because the next thing I remembered was Joseph leering over me. Somehow, I was naked, and he was doing things to me, using objects on me and posing me.'

Annabelle's voice broke into a hoarse whisper, the shame and embarrassment written across her face.

'I know what he'd been doing because he showed me photographs. I tried to fight him off, but he'd gagged me and tied my arms and legs so I couldn't kick out or push him away. I was out of it. Everything kept going black. There was no strength in me. I passed out again. I'm not sure how long for. I'm guessing it was half an hour, or an hour. I'd completely lost track of time by then.' Annabelle let out a shuddering sigh.

'When I woke up, there was another girl on the bed, too. She was also tied up and half naked, and she was unconscious. I was coming round more then and tried to shake her awake, but I couldn't. I tried to undo the ties on my wrists and ankles, but Joseph came back into the room. He pulled his trousers off and climbed on top of me and raped me. This time, he had sex with me. When he'd finished, he said that if I ever breathed a word of anything that went on at the dinner, he would share the photographs and videos he'd taken with the world, with my parents, across the university. I would never get a job. My father would be so ashamed. I remember crying and him sitting on top of me, laughing. His face was manic, like a madman. I'd never seen him like that. He seemed to be totally high on what he was doing. Then he said that if I ever felt brave enough to not worry about the shame, he would kill me. He put his hands around my throat and started to squeeze. I couldn't breathe, I passed out again.'

Harrison watched the young woman in front of him, reliving the horror of that night. It was taking every ounce of her strength to tell him, but he knew it was just the first tentative step on her road to recovery. He wanted to head straight back to the station and confront Joseph. His blood boiled with anger towards him, but he had to stay calm for her.

'Sorry,' she whispered as she tried to pull herself together, 'this is the first time I've told anybody.'

'Don't apologise,' Harrison replied gently. 'Take your time.'

Annabelle took a few deep breaths.

'When I came round again, all hell had broken loose in the other room. I could hear shouting. They were all arguing. I managed to loosen the ties enough on my ankles to undo them and get up. I couldn't dress, couldn't free my hands, but I peered around the door and I saw him, Christopher. I could tell he was dead. He was lying naked in some kind of coffin box. I think they'd been hitting him with sticks because he had bruises all over him, and I could hear them saying they shouldn't have put him in the box, that something had gone wrong and he'd died.'

Annabelle stopped again. Gulping for air. Harrison knew she was having a panic attack. For a year she had kept all this pain and horror inside of her and been forced to get on with her life as though nothing had happened. She was stronger and braver than she realised.

'Please take time and let yourself breathe,' he said to her. 'Count to ten slowly.' He waited, monitoring her closely. 'Breathe in and out. Focus only on your breathing. One, two, three,' he counted softly.

Slowly Annabelle's face regained some colour, and the whites of her knuckles turned to pink as she loosened her grip on the duvet. Then she took a deep breath and started talking again.

'Joseph was calm, and just told them all to shut up and said they were going to have to get rid of him. I was hysterical. He saw me and just slapped me hard and told me that if I ever breathed a word, he would kill me. He told the others that too. Said they were all in this together. It was what the brotherhood was for, and the price of being a traitor was death. It was sick.'

Annabelle looked into Harrison's eyes. He felt pity for her, just twenty years old and she'd been exposed to Joseph Goode's sadism so brutally.

'I didn't know what to do. I must have been shocked and traumatised. The rape, Christopher. I'm not even sure how I got back here. When I was told that Christopher was missing, I think they all thought that's why I was upset. I could barely look at his parents. I wanted to speak out, really I did. I even walked to the police station one day, but I was just so scared. What if they didn't believe me? I knew that all of them had rich families. They'd be able to afford really good lawyers and you hear these stories... My parents aren't wealthy, and my dad hadn't been well. I thought the shock and shame might kill him too. As the months went on, I got a bit stronger and then I saw that they were carrying on as though nothing had happened. I had to do something. The only thing I could think of was to draw attention to where he was buried. I couldn't let Joseph know it was me, so I wore a mask and the cloak and hood. I put graffiti up around Moatside Lane to scare them, and hoped that one of the others might get brave enough to challenge Joseph, or at least that someone would eventually connect the Moatside Monks with it.'

'What about George?'

'I don't know anything about George. I don't care either. He was there. He took part in what happened. I know it's wrong, but I don't care. Maybe Joseph knew he was wavering, and he thought it was George who was causing the trouble.'

'I need to ask you if Joseph cut you at all.'

'Cut me? Yes. Yes he did. On my butt cheek, he sliced a piece of skin off, I've got a scar.'

'Triangular?'

She nodded.

'You might not know this, but did you notice what he did with it?'

'No. Oh God, has he kept it?'

'Possibly, but it would be evidence that could convict him.'

'Oh God.' She put her head into her hands and rubbed her face. 'He did it to Christopher, too. I noticed he also had a triangle cut into him. Although he was badly bruised, I could see the raw patch. They got him out of the box and dressed him in the monk's cloak. That's when I saw it. Joseph made me watch. I think it was to scare me. Maybe he also knew it upset me. He kept telling the others that he would protect them now that they were brothers for life. Joseph went out and when he came back, he told them about the rose garden. It had just been dug and planted the day before and the screens around the area were still up, so it was hidden from view. They knew where to get spades. There's a place the Castle gardeners used to store their equipment. It all seemed so easy for him and the others just followed whatever he said.'

Harrison stayed with Annabelle for another half an hour to ensure she was alright on her own. He promised her that they would catch up with Joseph and asked her to promise that she would seek counselling for what had happened to her. It made him feel sick. The abuse she had been put through. Joseph Goode was a sadist in every way, but his need for control and ritual would be his undoing. Right now, Annabelle was too scared to speak out officially against him for fear Joseph would release the images he had of her. But Harrison had another way to prove his guilt.

22

H arrison was on his way back to his bike when a text came through from Ryan telling him to look at his emails. What he saw made him stop in his tracks. After reading just a few sentences, he knew he was looking at the blueprint for a murderer, and, most importantly, the means to catch him.

Harrison found DI Steadman staring lovingly at a ciabatta roll he'd taken out of his lunch box. He'd only managed to have two bites from it when Harrison's bulk filled the view from his desk.

'Have we got the search warrant?' Harrison asked.

Steadman sighed.

'I would love to be able to tell you that we have Dr Lane, but you've seen that army of suits. We are facing an uphill battle on that one.'

'My colleague has sent me through a Child Protective Services report from America. I've no idea how he came to have hold of it, but it also came with a couple of newspaper cuttings from 2013. I'm guessing they'd been "acquired" by journalists. What they contain show that Joseph Goode is our killer, and I know how to prove it.'

'Go on.' Steadman placed his ciabatta roll back into his lunchbox and closed the lid.

'The report starts when he was just fourteen. Child Protective Services had been called in after several people had expressed concern about him. They discovered that not only was he an alcoholic, probably been drinking since he was eight years old, but he'd been brought up in an environment where drink, drugs and sex parties were the norm. He also had a string of sex attacks that were linked to him. No one would go on the record. All the complaints got settled before they amounted to anything. You have to remember who his dad was, and although he had a completely dysfunctional relationship with his father, and was immediately taken away and put into the care of his uncle, they still maintained contact.'

'What about the mother?'

'Died of a drug overdose a few years before. The uncle is her brother. It's tragic reading, but it's critical for this inquiry,' Harrison continued. 'It gives us some pretty big clues as to the kind of personality Joseph is, and he fits the profile perfectly. He was drinking heavily from an early age. If children and young teenagers drink like that, they can get a form of brain damage. You might not notice if he's intelligent, but it could affect the frontal lobe which has to do with judgement, decision making and critically, impulse control. It also impacts the amygdala, which deals with emotions like fear and anxiety. It explains why he appears so cool under pressure. Whoever killed Christopher and George is sadistic. They enjoy inflicting pain on other people and having power over them.'

Steadman was listening intently, not interrupting, and a couple of other detectives had heard the conversation and were also listening in.

Harrison continued, 'In the report, Joseph was also said to be showing signs of Satanic influence. There was the mention of a gang and of cats disappearing from his uncle's neighbourhood when he moved in. Also, that he subjected girls to a barbaric ritual whereby he cut a small triangular-shaped piece of skin from their buttocks. The father paid the girls off. No official complaints were ever made; they said they were consenting. George had a triangular-shaped piece of skin cut from him.'

'You saying he had some kind of sexual relationship with George?'

'No. Although it's possible. It's his ritual to show he has power over somebody. In Satanism, a triangle represents a place where a demon has materialised. I think Joseph sees himself as that demon and believes it gives him control over that person for life, a sign that he'd been there and done what he wanted.'

'So it's some kind of Satanic ritual or a trophy?'

'Probably a bit of both. I'm damned sure he keeps them somewhere. In his warped mind he thinks it maintains that control.'

'Would he be stupid enough to keep it in the house?'

'He thinks he's untouchable – protected, if you like. There will be somewhere that he hides them, perhaps even in plain sight, but definitely not far from where he is. He will want them near to him. They have to be there.'

Harrison could see the DI's mind working overtime. Most of the officers in the incident room had gradually drifted over to them, and they were now surrounded by the majority of the team.

'We're going to have to be smart and quick. They're going to come down on us like a ton of bricks. If I get the warrant, we need to be ready to go in immediately because they'll attempt to get it withdrawn. There'll be no time to lose. The families and their lawyers will challenge it the instant they know about it. We will have just minutes to get in there and find that evidence.'

'I'll get onto the tactical unit straight away, boss,' Urquhart said.

'I'll alert Forensics,' Emily added.

Harrison could see the adrenaline pumping through every one of them. This was the moment they'd all be working towards.

It took DI Steadman four nerve-wracking hours to persuade his boss, and then the courts, that a search warrant was justified and speed was essential. Their evidence was tentative, and he knew they'd only just got it past the court process. It wouldn't take much to overturn it and change the judge's mind. Joseph Goode had been arrested and sat stewing in the cells while the rest of his gang were released pending further enquiries. Steadman used the four hours wisely, making sure they were prepped, so they had the best team for the job ready to go in the second they had the warrant. Harrison briefed everyone on what to look for and who their main suspect was.

'Forensics should focus on the main living room area. There may be blood traces from Christopher Downey there. We need to see if we can find the sticks that they used to beat initiates, although they may not have been stupid enough to keep them at the house. The monk cloaks too, but again, if they have any sense, they'll have moved these already. The primary suspect is Joseph Goode. I believe he has trophies from his victims stored somewhere, probably in his room. These are tiny pieces of human skin.' Harrison watched the lips of his audience curl up in disgust. 'They will obviously be dried out, but were triangular-shaped. That is our key piece of evidence because in amongst those pieces of skin, I believe we will find one from both Christopher and George. We have to find those trophies.'

'We've got officers watching the house already so if the lads who have been sent home decide to clear any evidence, we will be on to them.' DI Steadman said to the team. 'You need to go in too, Harrison,' he added. 'This is your specialism and, if I'm right, we are going to have a maximum of half an hour to forty-five minutes before the court suspends the warrant. There will be the full firing power of five crack law teams on this. The families are going to do everything in their power to cry harassment. If we don't find anything to give us enough evidence to bring charges, then we are going to be up shit creek without a boat, let alone a paddle. This is a gamble that has to pay out.'

Harrison travelled with the tactical unit deployed to gain access to the property. DI Steadman stayed behind monitoring the operation and in full communication with Sergeant Bob Wilson, who was leading the operation on the ground. Steadman was also ready and waiting for the inevitable phone call from the court that would rescind the warrant and call a halt to the operation. He was ready to fight it with everything in his power.

Gaining entry was easy. They knocked. Oscar Whittington and his lopsided fringe answered the door. Harrison thought how Steadman, watching back at the station via the video feed from Sergeant Wilson's body cam, would have enjoyed the look of utter surprise on the student's face as he opened the door to a dozen white-suited ghosts. The entire team was dressed from head to toe in the white polyethylene hooded Tyvek suits, plus face masks and blue nitrile gloves. There was going to be no opportunity for any argument that evidence was contaminated. Wilson, who was in front, was also a bodybuilder, and with Harrison book-ending the team at the rear, they completely filled the narrow Moatside Lane outside the flat. The open-mouthed Oscar was served with the warrant, and they were inside within sixty seconds.

The flat was a large one in student terms, and furnishings were several grades above that he'd seen in the former miner's cottage with the rugby lads. A dining table dominated one side of the living room. It was also extendable for even larger gatherings, and Harrison thought back to what Annabelle had said about the selection dinner.

'Might be worth dusting under that table for fingerprints,' he said to one of the forensic team. They needed to be quick and specific about what they spent time gathering, as time was so short.

There were three leather sofas in the middle of the room, positioned around an empty space in front of the TV. It was obvious that something had been removed from that space, some kind of coffee table, perhaps the coffin-like box that Annabelle had talked about?

The flat was also impeccably clean. Quite apart from the fact they had a cleaner who came in, there had also been a definite attempt to ensure that no evidence remained.

Harrison feared they would find nothing to incriminate the students. Their legal team would have advised them to remove anything that could be 'misconstrued', and that almost certainly was going to cover the sticks they used to beat initiates, their monks' cloaks and any other ceremonial items.

The rest of the team swarmed around him, pulling drawers open and searching under cushions and in cupboards. Some of the forensics team were setting up their lights to search for bloodstains, and Oscar, James, Mark and David were on their mobile phones talking to their lawyers in a shocked huddle in the corner of the room.

Harrison stopped and stood still. There was so much activity and noise, it was almost impossible to concentrate. He closed his eyes and summoned every mental effort he could to block all the environmental stimuli out and focus his mind. He had to find proof of the Moatside Monks' existence and Joseph's guilt.

When his eyes snapped open, he was ready to look. Like a scanner, he took in the whole room inch by inch. The dining table, candlesticks. Bookcase, pictures on the wall. The sofas, the missing coffee table. The room looked decluttered, spotless. They had removed all of their secret society paraphernalia long before today.

Harrison needed to find Joseph's room. There was one thing he would not want to part with, and he would want it in his inner sanctum.

The bedrooms were split over two levels. Every room had two officers in it. The team were being thorough and knew they were up against the clock. As he walked past each door, he could see white-suited officers sorting through wardrobes and drawers.

Finding Joseph's room was easy. On the door was a triangle with *J* in the middle.

Two male officers were in the room already, searching through his things. They had taken books off the shelves, opened tins and boxes, searched under the bed and mattress. Harrison started his own systematic search, just as a message came over the police radios.

'The boys' lawyers are petitioning the court for harassment. They claim they should be treated as potential victims, not suspects. We have ten to fifteen minutes max.'

They searched everywhere. Every book and ornament came off the shelves, every piece of floorboard was checked. The curtains. His clothes in the wardrobe, pockets, linings, shoes, even the heels of his shoes. The two officers finally stood up and looked at Harrison, beaten.

'It has to be here somewhere,' he said. 'They're tiny, easy to conceal.'

'We'll start again,' one officer replied, and the two of them set about re-checking everything they'd looked at.

'The judge is about to rule on his decision. We could have literally two minutes left,' DI Steadman's voice came across the radios.

Harrison's heart was racing. They had to find the pieces of skin. They were the only evidence that could tie Joseph to both murders and to his sadistic attacks on women, including Annabelle. He had to be stopped. Harrison could feel himself scatter-gunning the problem. If he was going to find it, he needed to think like Joseph, focus on how his mind worked. What was important to him? He stopped a moment and mentally went through the list of personality traits, his childhood history. What motivated him. Joseph's steely gaze as he'd interviewed him at the police station came into his mind. The look he'd given him when he asked how he'd got to be included in a group of the privileged classes with the others. The words of the American reporter, *He was obsessed with feelings of inferiority because of where his dad had come from and where their money was made.*

Then it clicked. It was staring right at him.

He'd glanced at it on the bookshelf when he'd entered the room. Seen it discarded on the bed. It had already been checked, but the image of pressed flowers between a book's pages came into Harrison's mind. It was a big, thick hardback. If you'd pressed something between its pages, you wouldn't necessarily see that as you flicked through to check it had nothing hidden inside.

'The court warrant has been recalled. We have to pull out.' DI Steadman's voice barely made it into Harrison's mind. He was walking towards Joseph's bed, where the books were piled after being pulled off the shelves. He could just see it, the red and gold of *Debrett's Peerage & Baronetage* showing underneath a pile of textbooks. He grabbed it.

'Dr Lane, we need to leave now,' one of the officers in the room said to him.

He didn't so much ignore him as simply not hear. He was so focused on his task. Harrison opened the cover of *Debrett's* and flicked through the book. Nothing. There were no obvious places where pages fell open, no unnatural lumps or bumps. No gaps.

'Dr Lane? I'm sorry, but we have to leave.'

Harrison wasn't about to give up. He lay the book flat on the bed and opened the pages. Then he had a thought. George Marshwood, Baron Marshwood. He frantically searched through the book to find the Marshwoods.

Page after page. Baroness Ludford, Lord Mackay, Lord Mair, Lord Mackenzie, Lord Marland...

'Dr Lane. We must leave.'

Finally, he found them, Baron Marshwood, and there it was. Secreted right into the tight spine side of the book, a tiny triangle of dried skin.

Behind him, he heard the officer exclaim. 'Holy shit, is that it?'

Harrison knew there had to be more. He could hear shouting and arguing in the hallway behind him, between officers and the lawyers who had arrived to ensure they were out of the building. Now he knew where to look, he quickly searched through the pages of the book for other pieces. The Downeys, there was another piece. Then another. They had him. This was the evidence they needed.

'Dr Lane, I'm sorry, we have been ordered by the court to vacate these premises.' DS Bob Wilson walked into the room, followed by two of the suited lawyers.

Harrison turned round and held out the book, opened at the page where George Marshwood's skin sat, dried and pressed. 'We've found what we came for. We now have the evidence that Joseph Goode murdered George Marshwood and, along with Oscar, James, Mark and David, caused injuries which resulted in the death of Christopher Downey. I believe that all five then concealed his death and disposed of his body.'

'What the hell are you talking about?' One of the lawyers lurched forward to look at what Harrison was holding up, but was blocked instantly by DS Wilson.

'Trophies. Joseph cut triangular pieces of skin from those whose lives he destroyed.'

Harrison placed the book back on the bed. 'I'll leave that

there for Forensics to bag up.' When he turned around, despite the face mask, he could see Wilson had a big smile on his face from the creases around his eyes. The two lawyers had visibly paled.

'Excuse me, gentlemen, I need to arrest your clients. Can I ask you please to leave these premises immediately as they are now officially a crime scene,' DS Wilson said and began shooing the two lawyers out of the room and down the hall.

Harrison breathed a huge sigh of relief as he heard the rights being read to the four students down the hallway. Joseph's obsession with ritual and his insecurities about his upbringing had been his downfall. Harrison would love to be there when DI Steadman officially told him the 'good' news.

On his way out, Harrison briefed the forensics team about the book. He also told them that there was a camera or mobile phone somewhere that had incriminating images on it. He knew that Joseph wouldn't have used his usual phone. They needed to find the images, otherwise Annabelle would never feel free of his threat. The evidence on it would also ensure that, even without the skin, they'd have enough to put Joseph away for a long time.

As he left and stepped back into Moatside Lane, he breathed a sigh of relief. Annabelle could soon get the counselling she needed to get over her ordeal. Joseph Goode wasn't going to wriggle out of this one.

23

When Harrison returned to the incident room, he expected to find everyone in a state of euphoria, and Steadman smiling from ear to ear. Instead, he found it in a frenzy.

Something was wrong. With the arrests of the students, they should now be collating evidence, interviewing, and preparing for charges. Across the other side of the room, he saw DI Steadman on the phone. He was standing up, gesticulating, angry. This did not look good.

'Harrison,' Steadman said as he slammed down his phone, 'Joseph is gone. His lawyer has friends in high places and got him out just before the court issued the search warrant. Now we can't find him.'

Harrison's stomach fell.

'He'll know the game's up, that we've found the skin because his lawyer will have told him.'

DI Steadman nodded.

'We've got an all-ports alert out. He won't be able to leave easily. I don't suppose you have any thoughts on where he might go. His mobile is turned off so we can't track him. With his father's money they might be able to smuggle him out somewhere off grid. We've got to stop him.'

Harrison didn't answer. His mind was working through all the possibilities. What would someone like Joseph do? He'd be desperate. Everything he had ever wanted would now be gone, and it would be impossible to achieve ever again. For him, his life was ruined. Over. He would be angry. Angry at the police, obviously. He'd want to know how they knew it was him. How they knew about the skin trophies. He might suspect the others, but he wouldn't risk going back to the flat.

'Annabelle.'

Harrison called her mobile. It went straight to voicemail.

A detective constable walked up to DI Steadman.

'Boss, we've had a report that Joseph was seen in the Castle grounds. Someone saw him taking something out of a locker and then leaving across Palace Green, but he didn't go back to Moatside. We have officers searching.'

'Annabelle Keyes. She lives in Owengate and could identify him in relation to Christopher's death. He's threatened her before.'

'He has?' Steadman gave Harrison a *that's news to me* look.

'Yes. I'll explain.'

'Get officers to her address, now,' Steadman said to the DC. 'Dr Lane, is there something you need to tell me?'

Harrison recounted his conversation with Annabelle. 'She wouldn't go on record, she was too scared. If we can get Joseph back in custody and find those images and videos, then I'm sure she will. But my fear is that if Joseph killed George because he thought he was betraying him, then he won't hesitate with Annabelle.'

'Agreed. We need to find her right away.'

Harrison felt a sense of dread, pacing the incident room while they waited to hear news. Every time Steadman's mobile rang, Harrison pricked his ears up in anticipation. He listened in to the police radios as search teams hunted for Joseph around Palace Green, and he stood over the shoulder of the CCTV teams as they looked for him on screen.

Fifteen minutes later, something changed in the DI's demeanour and he rushed across the incident room to talk to some of the team.

'OK, listen up everyone. We have reason to believe Joseph Goode is with Annabelle Keyes. Her neighbour saw her leave with a young man matching his description. She didn't look happy. We have also had a report that a young couple have hijacked a car. The elderly owner stopped to post a letter, and the pair jumped into the car. Maggie is pulling up the CCTV now. Harrison do you want to take a look? You know them both. We have the registration and it's being fed into ANPR as we speak.'

Harrison rushed over to the desk at the back of the room where he knew Maggie sat.

'Almost there,' Maggie said as he came up. She was scrolling through some footage. 'There, that's the woman pulling up to the postbox now.'

They watched the jerky images as the elderly lady got out of her car, leaving the driver's door wide open, and walked a few steps to the postbox. From the right-hand side of the screen, two figures appeared. It was obvious that Joseph had seen the opportunity. He was pushing Annabelle along, hurrying her. When they got to the car, he shoved her into the driver's side and then got in straight after. It was difficult to see, but there appeared to be a bit of a struggle going on inside the car. Annabelle must have been fighting back.

Having realised what was happening, the elderly woman rushed back to her car, but Joseph managed to pull the door shut just as she got to them. She banged on the window, but he'd locked the doors. Joseph pulled away quickly, and Harrison could just make out a slumped figure in the seat next to him as they sped down the road, out of view.

'It's definitely them. It's Joseph and Annabelle,' he shouted across the incident room to Steadman.

DI Steadman was standing over a screen where the Automatic Number Plate Recognition software was tracking the car.

'He's heading out of Durham on the A690. Get all the available cars there, now. David, you take Emily. I'll keep you informed from here on their progress.'

'I'd like to go too,' Harrison said.

'You're not an operational officer, Dr Lane.'

'No, but I'm a psychologist who understands how Joseph is thinking right now. You might need me on the ground.'

There was a moment's hesitation.

'OK, but you follow David's orders.' DI Steadman returned to the screen and running the operation.

The three of them ran down to the car park and jumped into David's car, with Harrison sitting in the back. DC Emily Mitchell turned on the blue lights and turned up the radio, and they sped back towards the city, and then out the other side, weaving their way through the traffic. None of them said a word in the car. Urquhart was concentrating on driving, and they were all listening to the police radio for any updates.

'He's heading towards Thornley,' a voice said on the radio. 'No visuals yet.'

The journey was agonising. How long could Joseph keep driving for and where was he headed? Did he even know where he was going? Had he already hurt Annabelle? From the CCTV, it looked like he'd hit her. Annabelle's pale, frightened face came into Harrison's mind. They had to reach her before it was too late.

'Car abandoned,' came through on the radio. 'Suspects are missing. We're on the edge of Hamsterley Forest; they've headed in there.'

'Shit. That place is huge,' Emily said, 'and there are caves and stuff in there too.'

'The boss will get some eyes up. We should be able to track them with the thermal camera.'

'Not if they go into caves, you won't. How long until the helicopter gets here?' Harrison asked.

'Don't know, maybe fifteen minutes, possibly longer. We're almost there.'

THEY CAME ROUND a bend and in front of them were two police cars in the middle of the road alongside a small red Fiat. David, Emily, and Harrison jumped out of their car.

'DS Urquhart. Any idea which way they went?' Urquhart approached the uniformed officers, showing his ID.

'No idea. They'd bailed before we got here. Could be in any direction.'

Harrison looked around. They were surrounded by huge trees on both sides of the road.

'Has anyone tried to go into the woods to find them yet?' he asked.

'No, we were waiting for back-up. We've called for dogs.'

'Leave it to me. I can track but I need you all to stay well behind, do you understand?'

'You serious?' Urquhart asked, looking incredibly impressed and incredulous at the same time.

Harrison didn't answer. He just turned his eyes to the ground. Annabelle was out there, and he knew that Joseph fully intended to kill her. They didn't have fifteen minutes to wait for the helicopter or dogs to show where they were – they'd be so far ahead it would give them a good half an hour or more lead. That's if they hadn't already made it to the caves. He needed to find them now.

'I'm not sure the boss will be happy about you heading in there,' he heard the DS say, but it was half-hearted, and Harrison was already striding ahead.

The first problem was to see what direction they'd gone in. He stopped and looked around at the undergrowth. There were two natural ways into the woods, not tracks as such, but breaks in the bushes which would allow a person to walk in. He chose the nearest one to the car. The bushes were undisturbed, no branches snapped or bent, and the ground was clear of any disturbance. They hadn't entered there.

Harrison walked across to the next possibility, and it was obvious immediately that this was where they'd gone. Harrison also had an advantage: there were two of them and Annabelle was an unwilling participant. There was plenty of scuffing on the floor where she'd obviously tried to resist being pulled into the forest, and one of the bushes showed fresh signs that somebody had been pushed into it, breaking twigs.

Harrison dived under the canopy of trees, eyes to the floor, and followed the two sets of footprints that led him deeper into the woods.

Joseph had about fifteen minutes' advantage on him, but with Annabelle, his progress would be much slower.

Harrison wasted no time. Where the tracks were clear, he ran, crashing through the bushes and ignoring Urquhart and the others' shouts as they tried to keep up.

He was also aware that Joseph could at any time stop or hear him coming, so Harrison couldn't just keep his eyes on the ground. He had to have every one of his senses on high alert.

He went as fast as he could, weaving through the trees. The fact there were no footpaths on their route was good. It meant their footprints. didn't merge with any other walkers; it was just the two of them.

Around twenty minutes in, Harrison stopped and listened. He could hear water – some kind of waterfall up ahead – and he thought he also heard voices. The other officers were a way behind, crashing through the undergrowth in his wake. Harrison strained to hear. There was birdsong. A wood pigeon.

'No!'

He heard it. A young woman's voice, not too far ahead.

He needed stealth as well as speed now. Everything Joe, his stepfather, had taught him came into play. Harrison was back in Arizona, tracking and hunting.

He carried on, but now he crouched down, a coiled spring ready for action, and used the undergrowth for camouflage. The voices grew louder. He could hear what sounded like a fight. Annabelle was telling Joseph to get off her.

Then he saw them and all stealth disappeared and was instead replaced with rage. Joseph had Annabelle pinned to the ground. He was sitting astride her, and she was trying to fight him off. He punched her hard in the face. Harrison launched himself forward.

Before Joseph could even register the big man hurtling

straight towards him, Harrison had knocked him off Annabelle and onto the ground. Joseph was winded and shocked, but scrambled to get up.

Harrison had seen red.

As Joseph got back on his feet and tried to get away, Harrison threw a punch that made Joseph's jaw crack and his head fly back, flinging his whole body a few feet away, back onto the forest floor.

He was flat out this time, not moving, so Harrison turned to Annabelle.

'Are you OK?' he asked, walking over to her.

'I think so,' she replied, tears streaming down her face. There was blood coming from her lip and he could see swelling starting around her left eye.

Harrison could hear the other officers approaching through the undergrowth.

'Over here!' he shouted, waving to ensure they'd seen him. 'You're going to be OK,' he said to Annabelle, trying to reassure her.

Behind him, Joseph was coming round.

'Harrison!' Annabelle said, a look of fear on her face. She was pointing behind him to Joseph.

Harrison turned just in time to see Joseph uncap a small bottle he'd taken from his pocket. He looked at Harrison as he pulled the lid off and raised the bottle to his lips. Harrison launched himself forward, covering the twenty feet between them as fast as he could. He knocked the bottle from Joseph's hand, but not before he'd already swallowed most of it.

He guessed what it was. It would be more of the Monkshood poison that he'd given George. Joseph had nothing left to live for now except facing justice.

Behind them, he heard David and the other officers reach Annabelle.

'He's swallowed poison,' he shouted back to them, but didn't wait for a response. He grabbed Joseph by the collar of his jacket and dragged him towards the sound of water.

'You are not going to die. You are going to face the justice you deserve,' he said as he dragged him through the trees.

Joseph could die before the ambulance reached them and Harrison knew that. He needed to get as much of the poison out of Joseph's system as possible by washing his mouth out and inducing vomiting. The only way Harrison could do it, without getting his hand bitten, was to get large quantities of fluid in him, which would make him feel sick and dilute the poison as he did so. It might not be textbook poison treatment, but it was his only option until the paramedics arrived.

Within about fifty yards, they arrived at what would have, under other circumstances, been a beautiful natural waterfall and pool, surrounded by rocks and trees. Right now, Harrison didn't see its beauty. It was simply a means to an end.

He dragged Joseph to the edge of the pool and, putting one hand over his nose to squeeze his nostrils closed while holding his jaw open with the other hand, plunged him back first into the water. Joseph screamed in pain from his broken jaw as he went under. Harrison knew what he was doing was risky. He had to get enough water in Joseph to make him retch but not so much as to drown him.

Harrison held him under, the image of Joseph pinning Annabelle to the forest floor in his mind. A part of him wanted to keep holding him, but he didn't. He yanked Joseph out and then flung him on the floor and pushed his knee into Joseph's solar plexus. Joseph retched involuntarily, coughing and throwing up the water.

Harrison repeated it all again. Flipping Joseph backwards and filling his mouth with the water.

Behind him, he heard the sound of police radios and crashing feet. As he pulled Joseph out of the water and flipped him back onto his stomach and made him retch again, David Urquhart reached him.

'Harrison, stop!' he shouted.

'He's swallowed poison. I'm not drowning him, I'm saving him,' Harrison said to the panicked detective who had grabbed one of his arms. 'We need an ambulance. It will be his heart that's going to be affected. Find out if there's a defibrillator anywhere near, just in case he goes into arrest. I think he's swallowed Monkshood, the same as he gave George.'

Harrison wasn't sure who looked more shocked, Joseph or Urquhart, but the detective did as he was told.

Joseph moaned, he was beaten. Harrison dragged him away from the water and put the student on his side in the recovery position. The poison was starting to have an effect, and the fight had gone out of him.

Urquhart returned to stand with Harrison. 'Ambulance is on its way,' he said.

'You'll find a small bottle that contained poison back where Annabelle was. I'm pretty sure it's going to be Monkshood, but the ambulance crew will need that for Toxicology just in case, as well as us needing it for evidence.'

Urquhart sent two of the officers back to look for it, as a helicopter and sirens sounded in the distance.

'You checked in case he's got any more?' the DS asked.

Harrison shook his head.

The DS knelt down beside the moaning Joseph and searched through his pockets. He pulled out a small padded envelope and peered inside.

'It's a mobile phone,' he said to Harrison.

'That must be what he got from the locker. He gets his victims to stay silent by taking compromising photographs and videos which he threatens to share. That's probably what he uses to record them.'

Harrison sat back on his heels now, suddenly tired. The adrenaline was disappearing. Through the trees, he saw Annabelle being supported by a uniformed officer. She would be OK now. She'd get the victim support she needed and Christopher's family would get their answers.

Urquhart read Joseph his rights. The student was regaining his senses again, and so Urquhart cuffed him, just in case he decided to try anything else. Harrison's efforts to stop him from drinking the poison and then getting it out of his system seemed to have worked. He didn't look great, especially with his broken jaw, but he certainly looked like he'd survive.

Harrison stood back up and went over to Joseph.

'You thought George was the ghost monk, didn't you? Thought he was the one betraying you,' Harrison said to him.

Joseph glared at him, hatred in his eyes.

'Well, apparently the rest of them are singing like canaries back at the nick,' the DS said to them both. 'They appear very keen to tell us how Mr Goode here has been coercing them.'

Harrison looked into Joseph's hate-filled eyes. 'So, looks like your little group is disbanded. You were never one of them and never will be. They'll close ranks and you'll be left as the outsider you always were.'

24

'Assume that the triumph in Durham is at least in part down to you?' Harrison was pleased to hear Jack Salter's friendly voice. It was gone 9 a.m., and he was still in his hotel room where he'd crashed as soon as he'd got in the previous night, shattered after the day's events and the hours of statements he'd needed to give. Joseph had been kept in hospital for observation. His broken jaw had been wired, but there was insufficient poison left in his system to do any significant damage. He was not going to be able to escape justice and they had him on suicide watch. They'd found seven skin triangles in his book, and the team was now working at identifying all the victims.

'Teamwork, of course,' said Harrison.

'Well, glad to hear you'll be returning to us soon. I just wanted to let you know something.' Jack paused. 'I received a safe deposit box key this morning from Freda Manning.'

An icy hand clutched Harrison's heart at the mention of her name. He was jolted out of his tiredness, as though somebody had slapped his skull with an iron fist. His nerves jarred at the very thought of her.

'You OK, Harrison?'

'Sure.'

'I've informed Sandra. We will get Forensics in to help us with the retrieval of whatever is inside. It could be the answer you've been looking for.'

'I doubt that... Freda Manning is not going to do anything to help me. It will be more likely to cause trouble.'

'I'll keep that in mind and also keep you informed, of course. I got an update on her condition: she's still going. They're giving her another two weeks yet.'

'OK, well maybe it's a chance for me to chat through what it is she's going to reveal to us then,' Harrison said sarcastically.

'Safe journey home, mate, and see you soon.' Jack knew when to call it quits.

HARRISON NEEDED to hear a friendly voice, and there was one in particular that he'd missed.

'Harrison, good to talk to you at last. I've missed you.' Tanya's soft voice filled his ears and curled around his bones, making him relax back onto the bed.

'Sorry,' he said to her. He found himself feeling emotional, and he heard it in his own voice. The stress of the case and Freda Manning had taken their toll on him in the last forty-eight hours.

'It's OK, we're both as bad as each other – so wrapped up in our jobs. But I'm looking forward to seeing you soon.'

'How was the black-tie event?' Harrison suddenly remembered that it had been last night.

Tanya's voice brightened.

'It was fun, actually. I'm a little jaded this morning.'

'Did you know many people?'

'The guy who took your ticket turned out to be someone I had done my training with. Hadn't seen him for years, it was fun.'

Harrison felt a tendril of jealousy creep its way around his heart. He admonished himself. He also hated the feeling. That's what relationships did to him. They made him feel vulnerable. He had to fight that.

'I'm coming back to town today, it's been a busy week.'

'I bet,' Tanya replied.

He hadn't told her anything about Freda Manning yet. He'd save that joy for when they were together properly.

'I have to work late the next couple of nights, but shall we do something at the weekend?'

'That would be nice,' Harrison replied. 'I enjoyed our day in Oxford, perhaps we can make a day of it again and tick off another bucket list item.'

Tanya laughed. It tickled his ears and made him smile in return. 'It's a date. Gotta go, have a good trip home. Love you.'

Harrison hesitated, shocked. 'Bye,' was all he could muster.

More silence and then Tanya ended the phone call. Had she meant to say that to him? Love? That was a big word in his world. Maybe she said it to all her friends. Some people were like that. For him it was a huge word, full of emotion and responsibility. A word of hidden nuances that was different shades to different people. Some *loved* ice cream and dancing, others *loved* their friends and their pets, and then there was the partner kind of love. The one that came with a deeper connection still.

He'd not really seen her socialising with her friends before. They'd always met each other alone, drinking in each other's company like parched desert creatures. There was a whole side to Tanya that he'd never seen. He knew the professional Tanya, the private Tanya, but not the social Tanya. He had to remedy that.

For now, her parting words had enveloped him in a warm haze. He liked the feeling. He'd deal with the rest of his insecurities another time.

HARRISON WENT to Durham station for one final visit to tie up any loose ends before heading home. DS Urquhart was sitting at his desk with a huge smile on his face, and a McMuffin breakfast was fast disappearing into it.

'Never knew you could track like that, you were awesome yesterday.'

'Thank you. I learned as a child.'

'Such a cool skill. Apologies for thinking you were trying to drown Joseph, you can see what it looked like.'

'I can and that's no problem.'

'Mind, wouldn't have blamed you. There's been a fair few over the years that I'd have wished to hold under.' Urquhart smirked at Harrison and polished off the last of his McMuffin. 'John's been in some big wig meeting. The university has sent all its top people to see what they can do to get the mess sorted out. All the families' suits, apart from Joseph's, are suddenly being incredibly accommodating.'

'I bet they are.'

'Yeah, trouble is, we reckon the rich kids are going to get off lightly. They're pleading victim status, saying Joseph coerced them and there's some evidence on that phone of his that he did indeed have incriminating photos which he could have used to blackmail them.'

'I hope they get to pay in some way. They were a part of his sick culture, although I've no doubt that he was the truly rotten apple in the barrel. I think you'll find all sorts of dark secrets when you start digging. He's the product of a dysfunctional childhood that unfortunately corrupted him, mind and soul.'

'Do you believe in all that stuff?' DS Urquhart suddenly asked.

'What stuff?'

'Satanism, souls, and ghosts. It's what you investigate all the time, isn't it?'

Harrison gave a wry smile. 'I learned very early on that there are evil people who hide behind religions, myths, spiritualism and all manner of human fears and hopes. I've yet to prove any of the cases I've investigated are anything but damaged people like Joseph.'

Urquhart nodded thoughtfully. 'Bet you'd like to experience something for real though one day!'

Harrison didn't reply. He just raised his eyebrows and tipped his head in response.

'HARRISON,' it was DI Steadman. 'Annabelle's downstairs in interview room three. She said she'd like to have a word if you hadn't left.'

'Of course.'

'Several other female rape victims have come to light on the phone footage. Joseph Goode is a nasty piece of work. He also filmed the hazing rituals. He thought that phone footage was going to give him power – it's actually his courtroom death warrant. He won't be getting out of a cell for a long time.'

'Is he out of hospital?'

'Yeah, unfortunately has to drink through a straw for a few weeks.' He beamed a smile. 'No come back likely on your little altercation as Annabelle has made it very clear her life was in danger and he was resisting arrest, so you shouldn't hear anything more about it. We've got him on suicide watch, but he's about to be transferred to prison. We're just waiting for his first hearing.'

Harrison nodded.

'Been good working with you, Dr Lane. Your reputation is well deserved.'

'Thank you, and you too. You've got a solid team here.'

Harrison smiled warmly at Steadman and shook his outstretched hand.

'Well, safe journey home. We'll be back in touch when we need you for court, and I'll keep you updated on progress.'

Harrison slipped out of the incident room as DI Steadman returned to his desk and the ciabatta in his lunch box. Harrison headed downstairs to the interview suites. Annabelle was in the room with DC Mitchell.

'How are you doing?' he asked her, smiling.

'I'm fine. I just wanted to say thank you, Dr Lane. I slept all night last night for the first time in a year. I am so grateful.'

'Good. You must promise to get counselling. Just one of the traumas you went through would be hard to deal with, and to have kept this all to yourself must have been a lot for you to carry. I promise, things will get better with help and you mustn't be afraid to ask for it.'

Annabelle's face creased, and tears welled in her eyes. 'I will. I promise,' she said, her voice breaking. 'My parents are picking me up later and I'm going home for a few days, but I'll be back.'

HARRISON RODE home on his bike, content in the knowledge that Annabelle would get the help she needed to be able to get on with her life. He also knew that Sandra would be driving north soon to see Gemma. The ghost monk sightings had all stopped after the press conference with the prank ghost, Martin Jones, and Durham city and the university had once more returned to their peaceful state. Harrison had flagged several of the ghost reports to the university welfare team because he was concerned about the individuals' reasons for their reports. While there had been lots of copycat *ghosts*, there were also a few cries for help from people seeking attention because they were struggling with their mental health.

As he headed down the A1, the feeling he'd experienced two days before, when he'd ridden this way, came back to him. What was going to be in that safe deposit box? He was convinced that, whatever it was, it wouldn't be good for him. When he saw the signs for Harrogate, he had the urge to peel off and go back to the hospice. A part of him was repulsed at the thought, and a part of him was drawn there. The rational, controlled part, and the tired part, thankfully, won.

HARRISON WAS RELIEVED to get back home to his Thameside flat in the Docklands. To walk into familiar territory and shut the door. He was more tired than he'd realised, and after a shower and something to eat from the freezer, he'd been grateful to fall into his own bed and sleep. Familiar smells and surroundings cocooned him, and as he relaxed the tiredness seeped from his muscles and brain.

He woke up feeling groggy and tired. He'd slept for nine and a half hours, which probably explained why. The optimum sleep time is seven and a half to eight hours, and sleep cycles come in ninety minutes. If you break into one, it makes you feel more tired. He also knew that psychological causes of tiredness were much more common than physical ones.

He remembered flashes of his dreams throughout the night. Chasing someone with no face through trees. His mother hooked up to bleeping machines that were sucking the life from her, rather than keeping her alive. Perhaps his sleep had been light, disturbed by the stresses in his mind. Either way, he was sluggish and slow. After a whole week of firing on all cylinders up in Durham, he took the day off.

He knew he couldn't see Tanya tonight, so instead Harrison arranged dinner with Andrew. He was looking forward to seeing a familiar face and falling back into the groove of his life. His old friend was feeling adventurous, and they were going to try somewhere different.

Harrison touched base with Ryan and filled him in on how the case had ended, thanking him for his help.

'So if that's what university life is like, I'm glad I never went?' Ryan's chirpy voice made Harrison smile. He knew only too well just how difficult Ryan's own early adult years had been. 'I couldn't believe the crap they were all going on about on the chat boards.'

'I can honestly say that is not what university life is usually like.' Harrison smiled at Ryan again over their WhatsApp video call. Harrison was on his sofa in front of the big windows overlooking the Thames and Ryan was in his favourite place, at his desk surrounded by screens and his mountain of snacks. It's a nice city. Maybe one day you will want to get away from that desk and come out in the field with me.'

'Go with you? Out of the office? Boss, I know you. You like to work alone.'

Harrison knew Ryan was avoiding mentioning his agoraphobia as the reason.

'You and I are a team, Ryan. I can figure out the stuff on the ground, but you found information that was critical to the case online. I don't really work alone, do I?'

25

Dinner with Andrew at a local Thai went better than the last time they'd been out. Andrew was sympathetic when he told him about the meeting with Freda and didn't say *told you so* when he said how difficult he'd found it.

At the mention of the safe deposit box, however, Andrew's face had clouded.

'I think you are right to be worried. You need to keep a close eye on that, there could be storm clouds coming.'

Andrew invited Harrison in for a cup of tea before he went home, and the thought of sitting in his mentor's study, surrounded by the memories of his student days, persuaded him. He was craving some security right now and Andrew was the closest thing he had to family.

When they arrived back at Andrew's house, he managed to open the door with no problem, but the keypad on his alarm was playing up again.

Harrison watched as he repeatedly pressed the code into

the pad. The beeping of the alarm was making him panic, and any second now the alarm would sound.

Harrison remembered where Andrew had put the portable keypad, and so he dived into his study and opened the top drawer of his desk. Sure enough, there it was. Just as he reached his friend with it, the system decided it had given them enough chances and they were intruders, so it belted out its alarm.

Andrew was able to quickly shut it off with the keypad, but because it was monitored, he had to get on the phone straight away to the monitoring team to give the password and confirm it was a false alarm.

While he dealt with the alarm company, Harrison took the keypad back to the desk and was about to push the drawer closed when something caught his eye. He hadn't meant to pry, and there was a part of him that wished he hadn't, but the photograph seized his attention and once he'd seen it, he couldn't un-see it. He picked it up, his heart pounding in his chest.

Harrison stared at the photograph in his hand. It was clearly well-loved. Picked up hundreds, if not thousands of times over the years. He recognised all the people in it because one of them was Andrew, one of them was him, but he was just five or six years old, and the other person was his mother. It must have been taken shortly before they went to America.

Andrew had finished his phone call and walked into the room. As Harrison looked up, he saw the panic on his friend's face.

'Harrison, let me explain.'

'What is this? You've been lying to me all along. You knew my mother. Are you working with the Mannings?' The questions tumbled out of Harrison. He wanted to know the answer to every one of them immediately.

'No, no, I promise you, I'm not working with them. But yes, I knew your mother – and you – before we met at King's.'

'I can't believe that you've lied to me all these years. I trusted you. I thought we were friends.'

'I haven't lied, I just didn't tell you everything. Your mother asked me to look out for you. I was very fond of her. She was a beautiful woman inside and out, and she loved you so much. She would have done anything to protect you.'

Harrison was reeling. The room swayed, and he reached out for the desk to steady himself. He sat in Andrew's desk chair, leaning forward, his arms on his legs. He couldn't even bear to look at him.

'How did you meet?'

'I was young, just starting out on my studies and I joined their group thinking I'd get a summer of experience, that perhaps I would be able to write my dissertation on them, but it wasn't that easy. It was hard to get away from them.'

'Were you there that night in Nunhead?'

'No. I had managed to escape by then. My parents helped; they paid the Mannings off, got them to leave me alone. I didn't lose contact with your mother, though. I begged her to escape with me, but it was complicated for her. After Nunhead, she was in a terrible state. I helped her get out of the country.'

'You know, I've been searching for answers all this time. Why didn't you tell me any of this before?' Harrison looked up at him now.

'I don't have the answers you're seeking. What happened to your mother, or what happened that night in Nunhead. I thought about telling you I knew her, but she'd begged me to keep an eye out for you and I thought you might be angry, and that if you knew you would cut ties. I valued our friendship; I didn't want to lose it.'

'So, do you know why we came back? Why did she bring us back and return to the Mannings? If she asked you to look out for me, then you must have kept in contact.'

Andrew nodded sadly. 'Distance didn't give her the freedom she had hoped for. They had influence, and they knew who your mother cared about.'

'My grandparents?'

Andrew shook his head. 'You and I think perhaps your father.'

'You know my father?'

'No. Your mother wouldn't share his identity. I never knew him. You were born by the time I met your mother and joined the group. But the Mannings had some kind of leverage over you and her, and told her that if she didn't do as they wanted, then they would use it.'

'Why? Why go to all those lengths, what did they get out of it?'

'Control. They were all about control.'

'That it? Just some weird bloody control game?'

Andrew looked away.

'There's something else, isn't there?'

His friend looked Harrison in the eyes. He could see the turmoil in them.

'Tell me,' Harrison said to him, almost growling. 'You owe me that much.'

Andrew looked away again, scrubbing at his face with his hands.

'Andrew, tell me!' Harrison commanded.

'You. They wanted you. They saw you as their successor.

They didn't have their own children. They were grooming you to take over. They saw in you a strength that very few possessed, and an awareness of spirituality which was far beyond your years.'

Harrison wanted to be sick. His stomach churned and his mind began to creak and scream as images that hadn't made sense before in his memory started to become clearer.

'I'm sorry, Harrison, everything I've done has been to try to protect you. That's why I encouraged you not to keep chasing the Mannings. They were out of your life and now you've brought them back into it.'

'I didn't. They found me. This game of theirs has to be played to the end.'

26

Harrison barely slept. He'd returned to his flat, angry and confused. For years he had trusted in Andrew, but their friendship had been built on lies. He was surrounded by shadows, ghosts of the past, demons in the darkness. He felt like a tiny boat on a stormy ocean with no sign of land. He woke with a headache and was grateful it was the weekend. He wouldn't be able to concentrate on anything today.

There was only one man who he knew he could rely on. One man who had always been there for him and already saved his life once before. Joe.

Harrison rang America, but it was Joe's wife, Stella, who answered. Joe was out working, tracking drug runners along the border with Mexico. The drugs cartels didn't stop for the weekend. She promised to get him to call Harrison back, and he knew he would.

While he waited to speak to Joe, Harrison decided to get out of the flat and get some fresh air. Riding his bike gave him a sense of freedom, as though he had some control over his life. He revved the engine and roared around the streets, wishing he was on open roads back in Arizona.

He couldn't help it. He was like a moth to the flame. No matter how much he tried to resist it, he had to keep on trying to find out. Harrison pointed his bike in the direction of Nunhead. To return to the cemetery and to the place where he knew painful memories were buried.

He walked with purpose, striding through the gates and up the approach path towards the chapel. Then he peeled left into the trees, where the sky disappeared and the undergrowth rose up around him. Past gravestone after gravestone, choking, broken, tipped, or flattened by nature, until he came to the place he was always drawn to.

The graffiti had gone, but he wasn't there to see that this time. He pushed his way through the undergrowth he had cut weeks before, not caring about scratching and scraping himself until he was back in the clearing under the huge oak tree.

It was dark under the canopy and quiet. Even the distant drone of traffic was deadened by the foliage. He dropped to the floor and brushed the leaves and other debris away from the big flat white stone in the centre. Then he went to stand where he remembered he and his mother had stood all those years before. This time, there would be no running away from the memories. He knew they were there and today he would let them out. Face up to whatever it was that hid inside of him.

Harrison closed his eyes and reached out for his mother's hand.

He was seven years old again. In front of him was Annette Ward. She was in a white dress, lying on the stone. He liked Annette, but tonight, his mother was scared so he was too.

Her hand shook as she held his, squeezing his fingers too tightly and making him want to pull away from her grip. His mother was staring at Annette, not taking her eyes away from her. He looked at Annette and realised her wrists and ankles were tied.

Another image now. He was closer to Annette, close enough to see her face, and he realised there was something covering her mouth. All he could see were her eyes. Wide, staring, terrified eyes. They were staring at him. Pleading. Tears ran from their corners and down her pale skin, splashing onto the white stone.

Harrison could feel his heartbeat and breathing increase, but he wouldn't stop. Not this time. He kept his eyes firmly closed. He had to know.

A final image now. He was still standing next to Annette, only this time he felt Freda and Desmond next to him. They were dressed in black cloaks, and he heard chanting and murmuring all around him. The smell of fear filled his nostrils, and something else, the iron-laden smell of fresh blood.

Across the clearing he saw his mother's terrified face looking at something in his hands, not taking her eyes away from him. He was holding something. Something cold.

Harrison looked down and saw a large bloody knife.

In front of him, Annette's eyes were no longer staring at him. The light had gone from them, and now, she stared only at death.

HARRISON FELL to his knees and vomited in the decayed debris of the clearing floor. This was what he'd been trying so hard to bury, all these years. This was why his mother had run, taken them to America. As far away as she could from the Mannings' influence.

He murdered his friend Annette. It was him who had stabbed her, sacrificed her for whatever purpose the Mannings had deemed necessary. Seven years old and he was a killer. He was everything he worked so hard to destroy.

He knelt on the ground, all energy drained from him. The bitter taste of bile in his mouth and disgust in his belly. Everything he had done with his life was the exact opposite of that night. He had spent years trying to escape the Mannings and their evil, but they'd found him again.

He stayed in that clearing for an hour, gathering his strength and trying to decide what to do. His phone rang several times, but he ignored it. He was in no fit state to talk to anyone.

Finally, Harrison gathered himself and walked away from the clearing and the stone, and out of Nunhead Cemetery.

He knew where he had to go.

Before he got on his bike, he checked his phone messages. Tanya was asking what time they were going to meet and gave a list of possible places they could visit. He didn't hesitate. He sent a text back.

Sorry, I can't see you at the moment. I need to deal with something. It might be best for you if we bring an end to this now.

She replied straight away, asking him what was wrong and if he was OK. He didn't answer.

There were also two missed calls from Jack, who had given up on getting a reply and texted instead:

Got access to Freda's safe deposit box. Contained the necklace you said Annette used to wear, plus a large knife and a piece of ripped white fabric, both bloodstained. Murder weapon? Sent to Forensics. Fingers crossed we get some answers and a DNA match.

Harrison already knew what the answer would be. Freda had played her trump card.

He drove up the motorway to Harrogate, not really knowing why and what he was going to achieve, but because he had to do something.

When he got there, Freda was no longer on the ward. They had moved her into her own room.

He could smell the rot as soon as he walked in. She was decaying from the inside out; her poisonous black soul slowly devouring her body.

He walked in quietly and stood at the bottom of the bed. Her eyes were closed and he could see her breathing was shallow and laboured. She didn't have long.

Even in her dying state, she could sense his presence.

Her eyes flickered open.

When she saw the look on his face, a smile curved her dry lips.

'Welcome back, Harrison.'

A LETTER FROM THE AUTHOR

Thank you so much for choosing Deadly Secrets, I do hope you have enjoyed the third in the Harrison Lane series. If you want to join other readers in hearing all about my new releases and bonus content:

www.stormpublishing.co/gwyn-bennett

I love writing, and I enjoy sharing Harrison's mysteries, but they would be nothing without you, the reader. It is a roller-coaster of emotion producing a novel and after a long day when the words have not come easily, it gives me a huge boost to get a review from someone who has enjoyed reading one of my books. So, thank you, I am very grateful to every one of you who gets in contact and leaves a review on Amazon or wherever you purchased.

I also want to set the record straight and say that I went to Durham University and there were no murders while I was there. It was a fair few years ago now, I admit, but it is a lovely city and a great University; and I met the most wonderful friends who have stayed with me through the (many) years since. So, please don't let Joseph Goode and his Moatside Monks put you off.

Finally, I thought some of you might like to know Dr Sunil Sharma's ginger chai recipe, because it sounds so delicious. You can find a copy of the recipe on my website, and also if you join my free readers' club, you will receive a free Harrison Lane short story. The story tells how Harrison first met DCI Sandra Barker, and their first case together. It's free to join and I only tend to email once a month with book related news and offers, so you won't be bombarded with emails. You can join my readers' club at www.gwynbennett.com.

Thank you again for reading my Harrison Lane series, and I hope you'll continue the journey with Harrison in the fourth book.

Best wishes
Gwyn Bennett

Made in United States
Orlando, FL
26 July 2024

49576107R00139